D1467252

PARADISE CITY

PARADISE CITY

A NOVEL BY
K. E. GREGG

AMANT HOUSE

For Mom, Dad, and Robbie

K. E. Gregg lives and writes by the beach in Los Angeles. Born in Washington, D.C., she is a graduate of Duke University with a J.D. from the UCLA School of Law. *Paradise City* is her debut novel. She believes in peace, love, and kindness.

Flashes

PART ONE

PART TWO

PART THREE

PART FOUR

"This place can be a paradise. It is now, for those who live it."

– HENRY MILLER

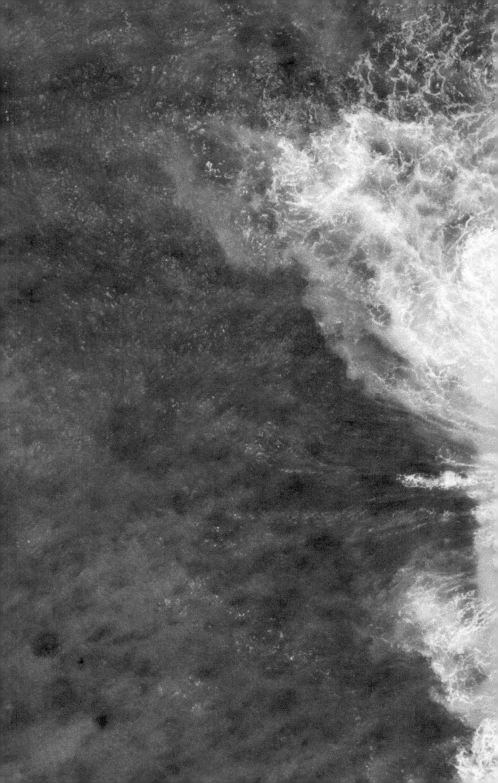

Part One

1

BLACK.

It's pitch black when the alarm sounds. I am shaken from a dream—a concert, I believe. To escalating chimes, I stretch, fumbling for the remote. At first click, I raise impenetrable curtains; light introduces day. I halt the chimes; my eyes adjust, focused on the ocean. Another click of the remote, a shuffle, Yacht Rock plays.

"Rich Girl."

Tap, tap, tap, I raise the volume. Hall & Oates fill the house speakers, singing me from bed. On tiptoe, I dance to the kitchen, brushing my hands against silk pajamas. At the fridge, I open both doors, letting coolness tingle my skin. A thought flashes, so I move on, through the great room, to the wine wall. *Champagne,* I decide, so I select a bottle from the chilled section, and I admire the vintage label before setting it atop the bar. Growing giddy, I slice the foil; I untwist the cage; I unleash the cork. *POP.* The bottle rushes open. At once, I draw the overflow to my lips. A long, sensational sip. Afterward, I zip the bottle into a koozie, *Sorry for Partying.* A few sips later it's paired with donuts, glazed. I lick my fingertips.

Sunday Funday.

Mid-bottle, I return to the master bedroom for a eucalyptus steam shower. Lost in thought, I twist a stack of diamonds up my ring finger. Time lapses; I towel off; I tie the strings of a tiny bikini. Awaiting girlfriends, I commence hair and makeup. All the while, I am sipping Champagne to soft coastal rock.

Near noon, another thought flashes, so I head to the study. There, I pass leather-bound books: *Contracts, Constitutional Law, Property.* At the end, I find my captain's hat, the one I wear on our Duffy, our sailboat, our yacht. I even wore it on the party bus to my law school graduation. Amused, I place the hat on my head; I adjust my hair; the doorbell rings.

"Grace!" My girlfriends enter, dressed in shades of Neiman's.

"Come in!" I hug each one. "Champagne?"

"Please!" one answers.

"Bubbles with our bubbles?" another suggests, fishing Adderall from her Goyard tote.

"Why not?" I clap my hands, and we head for the wine wall.

Already buzzing, I pop a second vintage. This time, I line up crystal flutes. When they're full, we each take an Adderall, untwisting the capsules, and dashing borrowed prescription into our drinks. Once complete, we indulge.

"Cheers!"

Somehow, in all my schooling, I avoided Adderall, even for the bar exam. In fact, I never developed a taste for drugs, until lately. *Just pills,* I tell myself, sipping bubbles with my bubbles. *Just pills.*

"Fresh air?" someone asks.

"Sure," I pull open wall-to-wall glass; inside becomes outside, and the beach erupts.

"SURPRISE!"

2

IT'S THE BLUE BOOK OF LOS ANGELES.

Spilled across the sand, fifty, seventy-five friends in swimwear, raising Solo cups. I see balloons, tents, a DJ, all framing the beach volleyball court. Truly shocked, I clasp my mouth, bouncing in place. Soon, we join the scene. Instantly, I am escorted to buried kegs. "Like Christmas!" I applaud my neighbors' law-defying efforts. "Hold my hat," I ask a girl-friend. "Gentlemen," I greet my guy friends, the ones I've known since Duke. "G!" They lift my legs in the air; I take the tap to my lips. "One, two, three . . ." they chant; ". . . fourteen, fifteen, sixteen . . ." they continue; ". . . twenty-nine, thirty, thirty-one" they finish. "Queen!" someone shouts, causing me to blush. For years, this has been my bit, a keg stand that lasts my age.

Always a crowd-pleaser.

Politely, I wipe beer from my face, and a neighbor introduces his fla-vor of the month. She's young. I think she goes to USC.

"Happy birthday!" He hugs me off my feet.

"Thank you." I meet his date, whose doe eyes wonder, "Where's your husband?"

"Oh." I pause. "He's traveling."

"Ohhh," she replies, no poker face.

"Aren't they cool?" My neighbor rubs her back. "They're the coolest couple I know."

"Thank you," I buy in, flattered. I start to explain myself, my husband, why we're cool; fortunately, I'm interrupted by music. The DJ spins Drake, Lil Wayne.

"The Motto."

On the song's opening, friends call my attention to a gift. It's a cushy plaid sofa, in the sand. I *love* to dance on a sofa . . . usually, at after-hours spots or late-night house parties—but now, in broad daylight. My heart swells; I run; I jump; I dance on that sofa. Immediately, someone passes me a bottle. I shake the bottle; the chorus hits.

I spray Champagne.

Friends laugh; friends cheer. Everybody's dancing—collective efferves-cence. The party is perfect. Manhattan Beach, breathtaking. Even so, my jaw clenches. I dance harder, but my heart sinks. *What's wrong with me?* There's this restlessness, a longing. My eyes water behind my sunglasses, and I stop, only for a second. In that second, it hits me.

I shake it off; I shake the bottle; I spray the rest of the Champagne.

"Love you guys!" I shout, but inside I'm disconnected. Out of place. Drifting. I've made a life of appeasing, pleasing. *Does anyone really know me? See me?* I can't tell. *Forget it,* I try to convince myself, up high, above my party. But I can't. So, I surrender.

My jaw unclenches; I acknowledge the pain beneath my sparkling surface.

I've never felt so alone.

3

SUNDOWNERS.

Cocktail hour, a progression from beach party to bar. Shellback Tavern.

I check my phone. No calls. No messages. He must be busy.

I need a moment to myself, so I seek solace in a bathroom stall. For a while, I'm on my own. Abruptly, a group enters. It's my group, and yet, for whatever reason, I stay silent, in the stall.

Quite drunk, the girls use the mirror. They start with lip gloss, then they resume conversation.

"She's out of hand," the first says.

"Totally," a second agrees.

"It's way more partying than before, right?" the first elaborates.

"It is," a third chimes in. "I thought she wanted to run for Congress?"

"She *did*," a fourth gossips.

"What happened?" the third asks.

"They told her to have kids first," the fourth says.

"Who's *they*?" the third asks.

"I don't know"—the fourth laughs—"the powers who decide these things?"

They're talking about me.

"Should we say something?" The second sounds sincere.

They stop talking.

"Of course," the first says.

"Of course," the fourth echoes, "but . . . isn't it kind of nice to watch her fall?"

To their laughter, I shudder. To their laughter, they exit.

Bathroom vacant, I leave the stall, part devastated, part relieved. "Fuck it," I say to myself in the smudged mirror. They're right; I am falling, out of perfection, out of pleasing, out of conformity. "Fuck it," I repeat. *If I'm not fooling them, why keep fooling myself?* "I'm exhausted." I shake my head, tempted by pity. Then, something in my core activates, and I return to my reflection.

"Enough."

I braid my hair beneath my captain's hat; I nod to myself, and I return to the bar. *Liquor*, I decide, but my path is blocked by sunburned bros. Determined, I place my hands on my hips, searching for an opening. In that instant, I am swept off my feet, one fluid motion onto massive shoulders.

"Need a lift?" I'm asked.

Towering above the mayhem, I laugh, at ease.

"To the bar," I request, wrapping my legs for support, as trained in ballet.

"My pleasure," he answers; ready, steady, and we go. I've been liberated by a gentle, shirtless stranger. Calmly, he moves forward, parting the seas. And without force, we reach the bar, where he lowers me.

"Better?" he asks.

"Much," I beam.

"What'll it be?"

"A Fanta bomb, please."

"Genius." He stands tall; the owner appears, and soon, we make introductions over plastic shot glasses.

"Wes." He smiles. The stranger becomes a friend.

"Grace."

"How befitting." He touches his shot to my shot. We drink.

"Dig the hat," he says, as orange flavor lingers on my lips, my tongue.

"Thank you." I tip my cap in his honor.

"I'm a Navy man," he says.

"Oh yeah?"

"Yes. A SEAL."

From afar, friends beckon. Without hesitation, I wave them off. "One minute."

"Do you need to go?" Wes asks.

"Not anymore."

"What does that mean?"

I hesitate, before coming clean, cleaner to Wes than to anybody, "Well, my dear Navy SEAL, I'm finding that my golden life is actually gold plate, over plaster, and that plaster is cracking."

"I see." He locks eyes with me.

"You do?" My voice shakes into new territory, true connection, being seen. A wave of emotion floods me. "May I hug you?"

He opens his arms; we hug. A sweaty bar hug.

Afterward, he places his hand on my shoulder. "What if this isn't a bad thing?"

"What?"

"Brace yourself for a truism." He lowers his voice. "What if the cracks aren't your life breaking, but *you* breaking through?"

I'm stunned. My shoulders melt.

"Feel me?" he asks.

Still stunned, I nod, my lips parting as he taps his chest. "Go deeper." He's so composed, so certain, that I ask, "What's the secret, Wes? What makes you so confident?" He re-taps his chest. "It's in here."

On those words, the bar fades away; I sober into clarity. "You may have just changed my life."

"*You* did," he insists. "I'm only the messenger."

"Thank you." I stare up at him.

"Anytime." He smiles. And in response, I give him my hat. "For the message."

"I'll cherish it"—he dons his gift—"until we meet again."

"See you then," I joke.

I slip out the back door.

Refreshed by ocean breeze, I walk The Strand, to a bench, for sunset. Around me, garden roses bloom. Pure white. There's a chill in the air, so I rub my arms, taking a seat to watch the sun dip, drip, into a navy horizon. The sky becomes purple, pink, and I hold out hope, for a chance. Maybe.

A green flash.

It doesn't happen. Not tonight. Even so, I'm struck by simple, natural beauty. What a contrast to my lifetime of excess. More beseeching more. More good grades. More achievement. More awards. More degrees. More popularity. More access. More status. More networking. More career building. More money. More clothes. More jewelry. More travel. More cars. More homes. More boats. More jets. More invitations. More memberships. More obligations. More wining. More dining. More parties. More pills. More thrills. More frills. More . . . because everybody's doing it. More.

To what end?

K. E. GREGG

Never did I question the formula. Instead, I raced a golden treadmill, up and up, never pausing, never reflecting, until tonight. Until this March, this birthday, alone on a bench, where I ask, "Is this life?"

Crickets.

Followed by emotion. Honest, raw, emotion, no longer suppressed by my well-rehearsed smile. Shame. Guilt. Fear. Anger. Humiliation. Blame. Worry. Hate. Pain. Shocking stores of pain, unladylike, uncivilized, coated with regret and despair. *How did I get here?* I ask, too nervous to speak. *I don't know,* I sigh, then, my thoughts shift. *I've had enough, and I am willing to change.*

Change what? My dream life. A dream decided by society, dazzling on paper, but debilitating in practice. For me. Longer than I care to say, I sensed it; I suffered it; and tonight, I admit it.

"This isn't me."

I'd lost my way. Celebrated, yet lost. The partying, the excess, the racing, all served to numb my inner conflict. To satiate some yearning. To fill some void. But it was unsustainable. Sure, if anyone asked, "Are you alright?" I would have deflected, denied. Deny, deny, deny. That's the WASP way. Radiant in public, restless in private. Even so, the truth remained.

This is unsustainable.

My thoughts spin; the sky darkens; I pull a sweater from my bag. I feel anxious; I feel uncomfortable, and yet, I stay.

Maybe it's the Champagne, the beer, the liquid courage. Whatever the catalyst, I get real. I face my demons. The sleepless nights, the anxiety, the migraines, the heart palpitations, the teeth grinding, the missed periods . . . all symptoms of a body seeking mercy, clamoring for change. For my health, I ask, *Is it too late?*

No answer.

I go deeper.

Is it possible to correct my course?

On that question, my discomfort fades; I'm no longer alone. There's a voice, an ally, perhaps it's my soul. It's coming from within. No judgment. No criticism. A single, soothing word. An answer.

Yes.

4

PERCOCET.

From revelation, relapse, incited by a brutal hangover. Sunday Funday into Monday Blues. Career on pause, having children on pause, I place a chalky pill on my tongue, and I swallow synthetic comfort. With Evian.

By the bed, a trail of evidence. My bag, my sandals, my bikini, strewn across the floor. Naked, I toss and turn between linen sheets, biding my time until . . .

The off button.

K. E. GREGG

Many hours later, the home phone rings. It's Him.

"Hey," I answer.

"*Babe* . . ." He says, "Sorry I missed your birthday. No cell service on the boat."

"No worries," I say, defaulting to cool. "I got your flowers . . . they're beautiful."

"Good." I can hear his smile from across the world. "How are you?" He asks.

My heart races. *Tell Him*, my inner voice suggests.

I freeze.

"You there?" He asks, "Babe?"

"I'm here," I return, feeling everything and nothing through the Percocet.

"Good." He's nervous. "Everything good?"

I don't remember starting to cry, but my cheeks are wet with tears. I'm not articulate; I'm not diplomatic, but I am honest, when I confess, "No."

He pauses. He asks, "What?"

"I'm unhappy."

5

TWENTY-FOUR HOURS.

"Twenty-four hours until the movers come," I tell my brother, Loyal. In the month since my confession, things escalated and unraveled, quickly.

"Let's do this." Loyal tosses me a Coors Light.

"Like a Band-Aid," I say, cracking the silver bullet. "Music?"

"On it." Loyal grabs the remote, and my dream house fills with Bone Thugs-N-Harmony, "Tha Crossroads." "Bless you," I say, my mood lifting. The song transports me to our high school house parties. The familiarity relaxes me.

Together, we sing, as Loyal strips tape to assemble the first box. "What are you taking?"

I survey my painstakingly curated décor. I shake my head. "I didn't get into this for stuff; I'm not getting out for stuff." I look up; I push through fear, and though I can't make eye contact, I tell him, "Just the basics, enough to start over."

"Got it." He springs to action as I raise the volume, tuning out doubts.

We pack; we pack; we pack. A whirlwind of dividing, disposing, fueled by dancing, jokes, pizza, beer. Finally, at the stroke of midnight, we're done.

"G?" Loyal calls out.

"Yes?"

His eyes mist. "I think you're brave as hell."

I fold my arms, embarrassed.

"Seriously." He blinks away tears. "I'm so sorry you've been hurting, but I'm so proud you're doing something about it."

We hug.

Loyal takes out the trash.

I start for the master bedroom, but I can't cross the doorway.

I sleep in a guest room.

6

MOVING DAY.

Bright, early, Loyal manages the movers, sending my basics to storage, until God knows when. Meanwhile, I return my car. A rare Porsche. Hands at the wheel, I marinate on how much I've adored my in-laws' collection.

When I reach the garage, I park; I tremble. Adrenaline courses through me as I walk away from the Porsche, clenching its keys. So far, so good, until their car guy greets me, "Gracie girl, how goes it?"

I burst into tears.

"I'm sorry," I apologize. I cover my face. Mortified.

"My goodness," he says. "What's wrong?"

"You don't know?" I shake.

"Only that you're returning the Porsche."

"We're getting divorced." My tears stop.

My world stops.

"My goodness." His tone changes. "Come to my office. What can I get you? Water? Tissues?"

While we walk, I'm on loop. "I'm so sorry."

He sits me in a chair.

"It's OK. *It's OK*," he assures me, with water, with tissues, before sitting at his desk.

"Really?" I blot my face, hoping to preserve my makeup, my dignity.

"Of course," he says. Matter of fact.

"Thank you." My world resets.

"How are you getting home?"

"Taxi?" I question my answer.

"Then what? Do you have a car? Of your own?"

I sniffle; I shake my head.

"That's right. Before your wedding, we sold it." He folds his hands on the desk. "Are you going back to D.C.?"

"I don't want to," I insist, "I know it'd be easier, but I don't want to."

"OK, then you'll stay in L.A." He cracks his knuckles. "That's set."

"OK," I exhale; I open; I make myself vulnerable to a car guy employed by my in-laws. *What am I doing?* I worry, but he continues, "If you stay in L.A., you'll want a car."

My tears swell. His voice softens. "How much can you afford?"

I shake my head. "I don't know. I'm not working at the moment. I have family money, but I'll feel like a failure if I start there. I have savings . . . but everything is in joint accounts. Frozen."

"Eventually, you'll have savings, a settlement, alimony?" he asks.

My chest tightens. "We'll see . . . for now, I'm focused on freedom."

"Got it." He nods. "Freedom."

"Not sure what that buys," I nervously joke, as my thoughts race ahead. "I do have clothes, jewelry, handbags, watches to sell."

"Good." He sounds supportive. "Credit cards?"

"Frozen," I explain. My leg starts tapping.

"Got it." He leans forward. "Grace."

"Yes?"

"I'm going to help you."

My jaw drops.

"Well, not directly," he qualifies. "I can't . . . the family . . . you understand."

"Of course."

He stands; he makes a fist, as if pumping himself up. "I'll be right back."

In his absence, I press my leg to stop its tapping. I finish my water. I force myself to read a car magazine. All the while, I repeat his assurances, *It's OK. It's OK.* Seeming eons pass before he returns, bearing paperwork. I lower the magazine, and he sits beside me, with contracts.

"Here's the deal," he starts. My face must have gone white, because he reaches for my hand. "It's good news."

"OK."

He releases my hand; he's back to business, "You still have a credit from the sale of your car."

I nod.

"It's enough," he says.

The tension in my chest dissipates.

He shows me the paperwork. "I vouched for you with the finance guys. They got you a lease. An Audi Q5."

I sit upright, like I've won the lottery. I pull my hands to my heart, in gracious disbelief. "*Thank you.*" The signing begins. It's happening. I'm almost out of body, watching my signature. *It's OK. It's OK.* The process unfolds; I have a car. The process extends. "Also, they got you an Audi credit card."

"You're kidding." My voice quivers.

"No. Not nearly the limit you're used to, but it's something."

"Why are you doing this?" I ask, fearful of a catch.

He takes a breath. "Grace, you've always been kind to me." He takes another breath. "Plus, this may sound crazy, but I had a dream last night." His words accelerate. "You know I'm no California Chardonnay woo-woo." I laugh, but he remains serious. "This dream, Grace, it's undeniable. A young woman walked into the garage; she needed help, and I was commanded to help."

Chills race up my spine.

"So"—he pulls my paperwork together—"I'm helping."

After that, we share a moment. Recognition.

When the moment passes, he drives me to my last night in my dream house. In the driveway, he reads a text from Audi, "Your car will be delivered at eight p.m. Don't worry."

"You're an angel," I say.

"Don't tell anyone." He smiles.

"Our secret." I laugh.

Then, I open the car door, and I formalize an ending.

"Good-bye."

7

WILD.

Summer, separated. My social circles, much like my assets, frozen. And so, I network by day. By night. By weekend. Friends of friends of friends, and beyond. A woman on a mission, to stay in L.A. to start over, with success.

Amply motivated, I dial up my charm; I lean on my pedigree; I secure access to another portion of the one percent. New faces, new places, and a plethora of invitations, granting promise, hope. It's desert getaways. The Hollywood Hills. Soho House on repeat. Ojai. Santa Barbara. Guest houses and hotel suites. Flings with an actor. A model. An actor/model.

It's wild.

If you're untethered, if you're single, L.A. boasts a bounty of pleasure, a parade of possibilities, including the Writer's Room, a hidden cocktail lounge off Hollywood Boulevard. According to the doorman, it's a nod to legends like F. Scott Fitzgerald who lived, wrote, and drank in L.A. Over time, I befriend the owners, management, who ground my transience. Somewhere, I matter. Somewhere, I'm a regular.

I belong.

One night, in September, I stop by the Writer's Room, and I hug the manager. By his side, I meet a man in black. He's older; he seems cool, and he's buying cognac.

"Cognac?" I ask, intrigued.

"It pairs well with cigars," he says.

"I love a cigar," my voice purrs.

"Don't hear that often. Where are you from?"

"D.C."

"Me too."

"Very cool."

"I think so." He pulls out a leather double cigar case. "If you're down, I have two."

"Please."

He orders me cognac.

Outside, on the heated patio, we sit in velvet chairs, surrounded by vintage rugs and flickering lanterns. "Harry," he introduces himself, as he cuts my cigar. "Grace." I thank him for the Cuban, placing it in my mouth, as he strikes a long wooden match. Once the sulfur burns off, I slowly puff, rotating my cigar around the flame.

"Grace from D.C. who smokes cigars," Harry narrates, before lighting his own. Soon, both feet of our Cubans glow. Leaning back, we cast smoke into the night, paired with my first cognac.

"Delicious," I think out loud.

"Glad you appreciate it."

I notice his skull ring, which leads me to ask, "What do you do?"

"I'm a director."

"Anything I know?"

He ashes his cigar; he shares the names of a few films. I remember, "You won an Oscar."

"I did."

"Wow. How does that feel?"

"Oscar's heavier than you might expect," he jokes, returning to me. "What about you? What are you into?"

"Well, tomorrow"—I take on a business tone—"I'm accepting a consulting job."

"Interesting."

"Why's that?"

"Didn't catch that vibe off you."

"I'm smarter than I look." I grow defensive.

"No doubt," he agrees, "but I pegged you for a creative."

"Oh. No . . . law, politics."

"A fighter," he says.

I laugh; he's way off base.

"Not at all," I say, as I pull in a mouthful of delicate, nuanced tobacco.

"Interesting."

K. E. GREGG

"I'm a lover." I release the smoke.

"OK . . ."

"OK what?"

"So, you'll be spreading love with this job?"

"Not exactly . . ."

"But you're excited about it?"

I shift in my chair. "Not exactly."

"So . . ." He leans forward.

"It's great money," I interrupt him.

"Cool." He eyes my Chanel bag. "Do you need the money?"

I look at lingering tan lines on my ring finger. "I'm getting divorced."

"Been there." He ashes. "You need cash, fast."

"Well . . ." I consider his statement. "I sold off my excess for a sizeable nest egg."

He nods.

He leans back. "So you want to prove yourself?" He's not judging; he's relating.

"Fuck." My summer crystallizes. I lean back. "You're right."

"Been there, too," he says.

"Really?"

"Yes. Want to know what I learned?"

"Please."

He sips his cognac. "There's *nothing* to prove."

My skin tingles.

He raises his glass, outward, to me. I clink his glass, and we drink. Afterward, he delves deeper. "So, what's the dream?"

I recross my legs. "That's the thing, Harry, I can't figure it out."

He senses that I'm frustrated, and he cares. His eyes are kind when he suggests, "Maybe you're overthinking it?"

"Definitely"—my shoulders drop—"my brain has been firing, nonstop."

"Your left brain."

"Excuse me?"

"The analyzer."

I cover my mouth.

"Yep," he says. "How's that right brain doing?"

"No idea," I tell him, through my hand.

He laughs, and by the end of our cognac, our cigars, Harry peer-pressures me into my right brain. Almost electrified, he encourages music, art, long walks, nature, books, daydreaming, imagination. Anything and everything to put me in my feelings. Our discussion transforms me, and before I leave, I decide to decline the consulting job.

"Doors will open," Harry assures me, before catching himself. "Just don't get caught in this bullshit." He circles his skull-ringed finger in the air. "Deal?"

I know what he means: the escape, the scene. And I know his suggestion will serve me, so I extend my hand, and we shake.

"Deal."

8

"GRACE ELIZABETH."

I know he's serious; he's using my first and middle names. "Grace Elizabeth, stay with me, as long as you like."

After leaving the Writer's Room, I phoned a friend, Jack. We'd known each other since prep school; we grew close in law school, but he and my husband didn't click, so recently, I'd seen him less and less. Even so, Jack dropped everything to meet me at Roscoe's House of Chicken and Waffles. There, we sat for a late bite, and I told Jack my story.

"This is big." He passes the syrup. "You need a friend, someone you trust."

"I know . . ." I agree, drizzling my chicken thigh, my waffle.

"I got you," he says.

"You sure?" I face him with teary eyes. I'm uncomfortable receiving help.

"I got you."

The next day, I park my Audi in Jack's garage. Wearing Georgetown Lacrosse sweats, he unloads my boxes, my L.L. Bean tote bags, my Louis Vuitton luggage, into his rustic midcentury Echo Park house.

"You can take my room," he offers. "I turned the second bedroom into an office; it's filled with records and merch." In January, Jack cut his big law hours in half to co-found a company, a vinyl record subscription club.

"Where will you sleep?" I ask.

"The sofa."

I pause.

"Thank you, Jack, but I'll take the sofa."

"Really?" he asks.

"Really. It's poetic."

We laugh.

A piece of furniture that used to be my party trick, my dance floor, becomes my sanctuary, my safe haven.

K. E. GREGG

That afternoon, Jack takes me to see a band at a block party. At once, I recognize the singer. He played football with Jack at St. Albans. As teenagers, we used to go to concerts in D.C., the 9:30 Club, the Black Cat.

"I can't believe this," I tell Jack. It's surreal, fantastic.

"Believe it." He smiles. Then, he wraps his arm around me. "Welcome back."

During the set, in sunshine, I relax. Apart from Jack and the singer, nobody knows me, nobody judges me. I'm free. For the second encore, the band plays a cover of the Rolling Stones. It's a song I've never heard, so I listen, intently.

"No Expectations."

I take a breath. The good, the bad, it's all transient. Where I was has passed. Where I am will pass. Given my uncertainty, my discomfort, I could rush ahead, but if I do, I'll miss the goodness.

"Having fun?" Jack asks.

"I am." I nod, telling the truth.

I am.

FORTY DAYS.

Forty days of crashing on a sofa, rebalancing, as encouraged by Harry. No contact with my old life, no racing to a new life, only a proper reset. Overseen by Jack.

Each morning, we run the Silver Lake Reservoir. Then, I make espresso, as Jack makes fried eggs and toast. While he works, I visit museums, parks, beaches, bookstores. At night, we cook dinner to music. Afterward, we talk or read, watch a movie or play chess. Then, early to bed.

It's mellow, simple, routine.

Thanks to Jack, I am learning to receive. No quid pro quo. Purely platonic. Truly receiving. No micromanaging. No over-giving. After asking for Jack's help, I am letting him help. His support eases my separation; under his watch, I am regaining vitality. Not by striving, but by simmering, by nourishing myself with healthy food, healthy entertainment, healthy activity. In place of proving or posturing, I am focused on personal wellness. Lately, I am inspired by a line from Hermann Hesse, *Siddhartha*: "*It is not for me to judge another life. I must judge for myself. I must choose and reject.*"

Choices are key.

During this time, my period has returned; I sleep like a baby. No migraines, no teeth grinding, calm heart, no anxiety . . . all signs of a body restoring. Simple, but not easy. I had to override years of impulse, indulgence. To keep me motivated, whenever I call my parents, Dad recites West Point's Cadet Prayer, "Choose the harder right over the easier wrong."

Choices, my way to well-being.

"Success," Jack beams on day forty. With blue pen, he marks the kitchen whiteboard. A final tally.

"How do you feel?" he asks.

"Grateful." I hug him.

"Off to the bookstore?"

"Think so."

"Go wild, you earned it." He laughs.

"I will."

At the register of Stories Books & Café, I balance my stack of purchases.

"Need a hand?" I'm asked by a man in line behind me.

"Wes!"

It's the Navy SEAL, from Manhattan Beach.

"You broke free." He smiles.

"I did."

"Treat you to coffee?" he asks.

"Please."

We find a table on the back patio. Over coffee, Wes admires my books. Then, we discuss the military, politics, philanthropy. I learn that Wes is going to New York, for two weeks, with a group of combat veterans.

"What's the occasion?" I ask.

"We're volunteering," he says. "Disaster relief for Hurricane Sandy."

"Wow." I finish my coffee. "How can I help? Fundraising?"

He thinks about it. He leans forward, placing both forearms on the table.

"Come with us."

10

DAWN.

Our red-eye lands; we deplane; we rent a Suburban.

Day takes shape; we drive through a desolate Manhattan. Outside the city, Wes treats me to his rest-stop favorite: Egg

McMuffin, hash brown, dirty chai latte. In the passenger seat, I savor breakfast. Meanwhile, Wes fills plastic gas cans, four, five, just in case. Back on the road, he lightens the mood with music.

Fists clenched, we sing at the top of our lungs, Zac Brown Band, "Chicken Fried."

All the way to our destination.

Rockaway Beach. November 2012.

Stunned, I place both hands on the passenger window. Unlike Wes, I've never experienced such destruction—battered homes, shattered storefronts, piles of cars. Aware, Wes pulls over; we exit the SUV. Without a word, he scales a mound of hurricane wreckage. Then, he shouts, "Come up!"

"I'm OK," I decline.

"Come up," he insists, extending his arm. "You're safe with me."

"This is scary, Wes," I say, before climbing, carefully, to his out-stretched hand. When I reach him, I grab hold, a firm clasp; and with one pull, he lifts me to the top.

"I made it!" I celebrate, steadying myself.

"You're stronger than you think." He pats my back.

"I don't know . . ."

"I do. Let's get your mind right."

"How?"

"How did it feel to scale this mound?" he asks.

"*Amazing*," I say.

"OK. Sink into that feeling and attach a word."

"What word?"

"Hmmm." He rubs his palms. "Hero."

"Hero?" I laugh.

"Yes ma'am. If fear creeps in, redirect your thoughts, your feelings to that word."

"How many times?"

"As many as it takes."

And so, I begin. *Hero, Hero, Hero*. One word, on repeat, as we return to the Suburban. "It's helping," I tell Wes. "Stick with it," he says.

We drive on. Soon, devastation gives way to inspiration. Among the wreckage, I notice spray-painted sheets: *You are mighty. You are loved. Never give up*. Following the banners, we reach the Forward Operating Base. Behind a church, beneath a tent, countless veterans organize.

"It's beautiful," I say.

We cross the threshold; Wes puts me to work.

My first assignment: mucking and gutting homes overcome by waist-high sewage. The stench is horrific. All day long, it smacks me in the face. Even so, I persevere, *Hero, Hero*, toiling through sundown, covered in shit. Literally. My hands cramp, my stomach turns, my body aches, but it's worth it. By nightfall, we've cleared the muck, readying homes to restore power.

My heart surges.

Back at base, I rinse off beside my team leader, an older Marine. Gruffly, he addresses me by my last name. "McLean, when you showed up, I thought, who the hell brought her?"

His blunt candor leaves me speechless. Silent, I wait.

Soon, he offers me a towel. And through his gray handlebar mustache, he says, "But here you are, covered in shit like the rest of us. Shame on me. You're one of us."

We shake hands, and he tells me, "Welcome."

For the next two weeks, that Marine took me under his wing, pushing me, guiding me, and on my last day, making me a team leader. At the end of my service, he tells Wes, "Strong recruit."

"Agreed," Wes says. "Thank you."

"My pleasure," the Marine answers, extending his hand, "Grace."

"I'll never forget you." I rush past his hand to give him a bear hug.

The Marine hugs back; I squeeze him tight, "Thank you."

At farewell beers, Wes asks, "See why I brought you?"

"Absolutely." I take a sip. "To see what you guys can do."

"No." He shakes his head. "To see what *you* can do."

I lose my breath. Wes's empathy moves me beyond measure. He sees it in my eyes, so I don't have to speak. Instead, I raise my beer; he clinks it.

"Cheers."

As we drink, a towering Texan approaches, with a dip in his lip, spitting into an empty bottle. It's Trey, Wes's friend since BUD/S, SEAL training. We enjoy some banter, some laughs, then Wes excuses himself to make a call. He's sharing the veterans' work with a former boss of mine, a U.S. congressman in leadership. During Wes's absence, Trey turns to me. "I hear you're pretty brave."

"You do?"

"Wes says you're going through some things." He finishes his dip, unpacks his lip.

"I am," I open.

"Change can be hard," Trey connects. "Not only that . . . it can be lonely. Old friends don't fit anymore; new friends haven't shown up yet. Man, that loneliness stings. But it passes. It always passes. Hell, Wes found you; I found you."

"You did."

Our conversation deepens, and a few sips later, we discover a shared loss. A SEAL we both knew, from different times, different places. At his name, Trey asks, "May I give you a hug?"

"Please." My eyes blink, fighting back tears.

He wraps his arms around me, and in our hug, I notice he's crying. I drop my guard. Trey's vulnerability triggers my own. Together, we cry, calmly. A cathartic release. Afterward, I dry my eyes. "What are the odds?" To that, Trey points to the sky. "You're never alone."

I look up, and without trying, I find my thoughts on target.

Hero.

11

"WHISKEY?"

Jack asks from across the living room. I'm back in Echo Park; it's December. I look up from my reading, *The Conquest of Happiness*, Bertrand Russell.

"We're going out," Jack says.

"We are?"

"We are."

I'm hesitant, but Jack serves Japanese whiskey. Neat. Next, he puts a record on the turntable. First song, I'm hooked; I stand on the sofa.

I'm dancing.

"What is this?" I ask.

"A new band. I thought you'd like this song."

"Big time."

"I'll add it to the playlist."

Jack grabs his iPhone; he adds the song to our shared playlist: Grace 2.0.

When the song ends, I sit down. "What's the plan?"

"A party," Jack says.

"Really?" I ask. "My last party was that block party. *September.*"

"'Tis the season," he says. "You're ready."

My iPhone buzzes; it's Loyal. "Heard Jack's taking you to a Christmas party. GOOD. Have fun!"

I turn to Jack. "You've got my brother on message."

"Yep."

"You guys . . ." My words trail off as I respond to Loyal. In that moment, I notice the date.

"It's 12-12-12," I tell Jack.

"Must be lucky." He sits in a club chair.

"Hope so," I say. "For a while, I thought the Mayans might be right."

"The Mayans?"

"You know, December 2012, the world ending."

"Please." Jack swirls his glass. "First, that's 12-*21*-12. Second, your old world might be ending, but you know what that means?"

"What?"

"A *beginning*." He raises his glass.

"You're right." I light up. My excitement builds. "What are we wearing?"

"It's ugly sweater," he says, eyeing my book cover, "but whatever makes you happy."

"Done."

I rummage through a suitcase; I head to the bathroom. When I return, I'm wearing black sequined leggings, a black top, black YSL boots, red lipstick.

"Watch out, world." Jack helps me with my coat.

"Ready," I tell him.

We enter the party.

"Flirt with someone tonight, OK?" Jack takes my coat. "For fun."

Before I can answer, we meet the host. She's a stylist, and she's lovely. In the kitchen, she serves us hot spiked cider. At first sip, a rescue puppy wags her tail at my feet. When I bend down to say hello, the host invites Jack to meet an investor.

"You good?" he asks me.

"Yes," I assure him, "I'll stay with the puppy."

"Cool."

Soon, an Australian accent joins. "You know Lucky?"

"Who?" I respond, still focused on the puppy.

"The dog." He laughs.

"What a perfect name," I say. Lucky rolls over; I rub her belly.

"Seems so," he says, and I remember my manners.

I look up.

I flush.

"Lance." He extends his hand.

"Grace." My hand is in his hand, and I'm seized by that magnificent warmth of chemistry.

"No ugly sweater," he observes.

"Likewise," I say, noting his white T-shirt and jeans. "We're rebels."

"We are."

His green eyes sparkle.

"Australian?" I ask.

"Caught," he flirts.

My heart celebrates. *I'm flirting.*

"Where in Australia?" I ask.

"Sydney. Ever been?"

"Not yet." I smirk.

"Well, you're a step closer, hey?"

"I am." I laugh. "Do you live here or there?"

"There," he says. "Only visiting."

"For work?"

"For sport."

"What sport?"

"Water polo."

"My dad used to play." I smile.

"To your dad." He raises his beer.

We toast.

Next comes the dreaded question, "What do you do?"

For months, I had given countless "acceptable" explanations. This time, my mind insists, *The truth.*

"Honestly?" I ask.

"Why not?"

Feeling free, a full smile comes on, and I tell him, "Nothing."

"Nothing?"

"*Nothing*. For years, I did all the things, but it didn't make me happy. So, I'm taking a break; I'm living on my friend's sofa; I'm starting over."

"Good on ya," he says.

"Thank you." I'm surprised.

"Was there a light bulb moment?" he asks.

I reflect.

Then, I answer, "I suppose I couldn't take another brunch of mimosas and gossip. Every advantage, and yet, this culture of comparison, complaining. It broke my heart. Soon, it took more and more mimosas to cope. It was a charmed life, but my soul was suffering. Inside, I felt empty, alone. That's when the light bulb came on. I could change. I could find a better way."

"So you left it all?" he confirms.

"I did."

"One fell swoop?" he asks.

"Onto a sofa." I laugh.

He's nodding, no words, nodding.

I divulge more.

"I think that's the missing link. I'm often asked why people at the top aren't better to those in need. In my experience, it's because they're fighting their own demons. They're unhappy. Think of a line at the grocery store. When someone cuts, the happy person says, 'Go ahead, you only have a few things.' But the unhappy person . . ."

"It's world war three," Lance notes.

"See what I'm saying?"

"I do . . . powerful case for finding a better way."

"Wish me luck," I say.

"Badass." He raises his beer.

I tilt my head.

"Don't you think?" He steps closer.

Necessity, sure. But badassery?

I look up at him; he's captivated. In his gaze, I reconsider myself. Not someone to excuse or explain, but someone to appreciate. "Yes," he answers his own question, so sincerely that I clink his beer.

"To you," he says, and we drink.

To me.

12

YES.

13

IT STARTED WITH A YES.

First, in Manhattan Beach. From there, yes after yes.

Tonight, tucked in my makeshift bed on Jack's sofa, I feel amplified.

Yes.

What relief.

And to sustain relief, I welcome the opposite.

No.

Full stop. No explanation. No justification. A significant stance, "No." Declining, refusing what doesn't honor me. Not only to reset, but continually. For years, I thrived as "the good girl." I'd grown comfortable putting others before myself. I'd counted on the acceptance, the praise, the validation. But those patterns brought me pain, and so, it's time to change. "No," I say again, aloud, committed. The word brings empowerment, a strength, which lulls me to sleep.

At sunrise, I awake with a start: December 21, 2012.

There's freshness.

Veracity.

I sit upright. A plan pulses through me: "I will follow my yes."

Still groggy, I find a legal pad, and in a stream of consciousness, I write terms and conditions:

If it excites me, if it inspires me, if it brings me ease, it's a yes. According to this formula, I will flood my life with goodness. True, personal preference. Certainly, other conditions abound. Fortunately, I have a formative weapon. My attention. To bolster my commitment, I vow to form a filter, focused on what helps.

Will it work? Not a clue. Therein lies the adventure. The exploration. Rather than wallowing in problems, I will seek solutions. I will open myself to possibility. Wonder. Whatever the source. Rather than analyzing life, I will live it; I will connect directly with people, places, moments. Through these connections, I will find meaning. Purpose.

My path.

Will it work? I don't know, but I have to try. I've already escaped my gilded cage, why not keep going? I have the means; I have the opportunity; and if I succeed, I can pass it on. Once liberated, I will use my talents to light the way. To freedom.

Pure freedom.

Part Two

14

THE DRUMS BEAT.

Three, two, one . . . for auld lang syne.

2013 opens; my heart soars.

From a glowing booth, the DJ spins James Taylor, sampled electronically, over the ocean. Renewed, we sing along.

> *For auld lang syne, my dear*
> *For auld lang syne*
> *We'll take a cup o'kindness yet*
> *For auld lang syne*

I curl my toes in the sand; his Olympic frame braces me, lifts me off the beach and onto his hips. With ease, I wrap him in my arms and legs, as he moves his lips toward mine, stopping short. To preserve tension. Above us, fireworks ignite, bursting, fading, falling into watery reflections. He takes a breath; our smiles merge; we kiss.

"Happy New Year, Grace."

I lick my lips, which taste of his peppermint lip balm. Again, we kiss, then he lowers me. My bare feet sink into cool sand. Next, his teammates replenish our drinks. Champagne fizzes, flows, brimming to the tops of our gold Solo cups. Making a toast, he whispers up my neck, "Cheers. To the rest of your life."

Every cell in my being buzzes, prompting me to clink and drink. Bubbles tickle my tongue. My spirit warms. I lean against his chest to savor its steadied rhythm. *Ba-dum. Ba-dum.* By contrast, the fireworks escalate overhead, *pop pop pop,* fire. Beneath the canopy of color, I close my eyes, cementing the memory. The beach *oohs, ahhs,* so I return, gazing up at the grand finale, a fantastic explosion, accompanied by whistles, applause, and a slice of silence.

Smoke clears; he takes my hand. Our fingers interlock to his team-mates' roar, "Icebergs!"

Heeding their call, we cross Bondi Beach into Icebergs, the swimming club. There, a new DJ spins a new set, spilling from the owner's suite. Our group ascends, but he hesitates. "Wait." Pulling my hand, we approach the Olympic-sized pool, which borders the ocean. Over its barrier, white-capped waves crash from Pacific to pool.

Boom. Splash. Boom. Splash.

Without words, we stand side by side, absorbed in awe. I stare at the waxing moon; he kisses and releases my hand. Almost innately, he pulls off his white T-shirt, strips away jeans, and in bright boxer briefs, 6'6" of tanned, toned goalie dives through the air, cutting up-lit waters. No splash.

Down, he glides, before resurfacing, seamlessly. Flipping the blond hair from his face, he treads water, extending his wingspan. "Come on."

I consult the party; I pretend to object. In response, he jokes, "If not now, when?"

Duly charmed, I unzip my black minidress; sequins fall to the ground. On the DJ's beat, I hold my chest; I dance a few steps back; I let go. In black lace cheekies, I run.

I jump.

Into the water I plunge, where his massive arms retrieve me. "Not bad, hey?"

"Magic."

For a while, we swim; we laugh; we play in the pool. Celebratory. Carefree. At some point, he encourages me to float. Weightless. Like that, I stare beyond the stars, feeling space, as if nothing else matters. Nothing. Like that, life feels both infinite and brief. *Why waste a moment on worry, doubt, distress? Let it all be forgot, with lessons learned and beauty retained.*

"Get it, mate!"

A voice cheers, joined by another, another from the balcony. I break my float; he swims to shield me, but instead of shame, I slip off my underwear, inducing him to follow. Emboldened, we commit to our choice, and he balls our delicates together, hurling them onto the pool deck. Once he does, respect is returned. "Good on ya!" the team captain shouts, as two plush towels fall from the sky. Afterward, the guys return to the party, leaving us to us.

Entirely naked, I relish it all. The night. The daring. The freedom.

And when my fingertips wrinkle, he scoops me into his arms, swimming me to the ladder. There, I press my forehead to his; his green eyes widen; we kiss.

"Happy New Year, Lance."

15

SUNLIGHT STREAKS THE ROOM.

My lashes flutter to focus.

Day one.

On the wall, a Stanford diploma, awarded to Lancelot, a man aptly named to sweep me to Sydney. Beside the bed, a vintage copy of Henry David Thoreau's *Walden*. Nearby, a team photograph, Australian Men's Water Polo, London 2012. With a stretch, I roll into him, rousing ghosts of Champagne. I moan. Lance smoothes my hair. "Morning, love."

"Hi."

He kisses the top of my head; he offers salvation. "Water?"

"You're my hero."

"Hung over?"

"A bit."

"Only one cure . . ."

Sex. Swim. Brekkie.

Breathless, we finish the first leg; he reaches for his iPhone; chimes fill the room. It's Swedish House Mafia, "Don't You Worry Child." My mood spikes; Lance motivates from bed, into his Speedo, back with my bikini. The song builds. I dress in barely-there-black.

Lance raises the volume; I stand; I dance on his bed.

Post swim, we sit on a coffee shop patio. Lance rubs my thigh while I finish a crispy prosciutto, arugula, fried-egg sandwich with the silky foam of a flat white. In that instant, Lance's team captain, Ben, appears with an invitation. "Fancy a sail?"

Deferring to me, Lance cleans his Clubmaster lenses on his navy tank.

"When? I ask.

"Now," Ben says.

By noon, we fly through Sydney Harbour in the company of water polo greats from around the world. Italians. Hungarians. Croatians. More. Plus, me.

At the helm, Ben looks every inch the captain, and I see why he models for Ralph Lauren. Near the Opera House, Lance shuffles a playlist, landing on Styx, "Come Sail Away." He pulls me close; I lean against him, looking over the ocean when the song strikes a chord. Certain lyrics cause my sentiments to swirl, and safeguarded by sunglasses, I allow my eyes to water.

On the final chorus, I clench my fist; I sing with new friends—to carry on.

For a few songs, Yacht Rock raises my spirits. Completely contented, I hear Ben shout, "Grace"; he wants me to steer. Tightening my bikini top, I approach the helm. Lance snaps a photo; a rookie reacts, "Lady Seppo?"

"You mean, Captain?" I joke, brushing off the Aussie "term of endearment" for Americans. "Seppo" derives from septic tanks, on account of Americans being full of shit. There's a point there, but I hope to be an exception.

So, I ride the harbor. Windswept. Invigorated. Gleaming. The mist on my face makes me feel alive, and I cherish the momentum. Time flies, mythically, and we reach our destination: a lush, overgrown beach, where Ben drops anchor, and Olympians splash overboard like boys at summer camp.

"We're swimming to shore," Lance reports. "Make yourself at home."

Topless, I tan on the bow, drifting in and out of sleep, calm, relaxed, when solid footsteps creak.

"Pellegrino?" a man offers, averting his eyes. Touched by his chivalry, I refasten my top. "Thank you." Then, "I'm decent."

"Decent?"

"You can look." I laugh.

Respectfully, he approaches. "May I sit?"

"Please."

Even larger than Lance, he casts a massive shadow, wearing a dark

Speedo, which complements his dark features, most notably, a full, trim chest of hair that distinguishes him from the others, who are clean-shaven, neck to toe.

He hands me a bottle. I twist the silver top, and it hisses, spritzing me. A bit flustered, I wipe away water as he sits, extending his hand.

"I'm Vlad."

"Grace."

"I know."

His words pour out in tender baritone, through a thick, Eastern European accent. *He would make an amazing Bond villain*, I note, *apart from his warmth.* I feel unshakable warmth, radiating from deep within him. It puts me at ease, which ripens me for his question, "Is Lance your boyfriend? Husband?"

I lower my bottle, absorbing his subtext. Lance is twenty-two; I am thirty-one; and Vlad, though eerily ageless, must be thirty-five, forty. Leaning back, I share, "We're dating."

"You live in Sydney?"

"He does; I live in Los Angeles."

Vlad mirrors me, reclining. As he does, I notice a tattoo, elegant script up his right inner forearm. At my glance, he gestures a shot on goal, which magnetizes me. Entranced, I watch my fingers float to his tattoo, before recoiling, abashed. Softly, he laughs. "I don't bite." Sitting up, he removes his sunglasses, so I remove mine.

Facing each other, his intense blue eyes ask, "May I?"

"Yes."

Permission granted, he takes my hand and traces my fingers up his tattoo, translating, "Mind over matter." For emphasis, he keeps my hand. "Understand?"

"I think so."

"It's the key to sport . . . and life."

He cocks his head; he squeezes my hand; he lets go. By his confidence, I guess his identity. The one with the most medals.

"The key to gold medals?" I verify.

He laughs, a bellowing laugh. He nods. He taps his temple. "Focus."

"Tell me more."

Humbly, he resists, but when I hold his eyes, he shares. First, I learn that English is his fourth language. After that, with full fluency, he describes mind over matter. "I start with a vision," he says. "Then, I commit to a process. Moment by moment, I show up; I give my best. If I falter, I take the lesson; I reset. It's almost religious. No matter what happens, I maintain my focus; I keep my mind in the moment. It may not sound sexy, but so far, so good." He gives me a boyish look. "And sometimes . . . gold."

I smile; we continue talking.

Early on, a coach called him a natural, but more importantly, *he believed*. Year after year, he maintained this belief, single-mindedly, supported by actions. Eventually, he reached the Olympics. Again. Again. And again. By then, medals served as confirmation, not validation.

"I've been on great teams," he adds.

"Who share your mindset," I say.

"Yes," he agrees. "You have to be gold before gold."

Goose bumps cover my skin.

Vlad notices; he grins, then, to defuse admiration, he points to the water. "Look." It's the guys, swimming back, in unison. A force. When I stand to watch, Vlad folds my pareo, which he presents in a perfect square. Touched, I thank him, and instead of "You're welcome," he says, "I'll come to Los Angeles for you."

I blush.

The guys return.

We set sail.

16

BACK ON LAND.

We lounge in the grass.

The Domain, by Sydney's Royal Botanic Gardens. A music festival, Field Day. Framed by Lance's legs, I sip beer, as electropop bounces off a nearby stage. Spent by the sun, our group recharges, when a flash erupts. *Whoosh.* Vlad's arm sweeps across my beer, deflecting a coin into a rookie's cup.

Impressed, Lance says, "What a block." Meanwhile, a baby-faced hulk takes his beer to task, chugging madly, as Captain Ben chides, "God save the Queen, mate, she's drowning."

Gulp. Gulp. Gulp. Absolution. The rookie flips over his cup, retrieving the coin. Triumphant. Over my shoulder, Lance says, "The Queen's on our coin, if she lands in your beer, you skull it."

"Close call." I raise my cup.

"Vlad saved you," Lance says.

Looking left, I smile at Vlad. "He did."

Nightfall.

We gather by the main stage, front and far left, a section reserved for their towering heights. Roadies prepare the headliner; Lance hugs me. "You've got great energy."

Energy? Off the lips of anyone else, the expression would have defiled my WASP sensibilities, but from an Olympian and Stanford man, it stirs me. *Energy. Was that what launched this whirlwind? From a Christmas party in Echo Park to a month's vacation in Sydney?* I bite my lip; Lance rubs my arms. *Perhaps he's nailed it. The quality. The distinction. My draw to him. To athletes.* My nearest and dearest could field a host of teams. Soccer. Basketball. Football. Baseball. Tennis. Lacrosse. Now, water polo. To many, the draw is prowess, glory, physique. To me, it runs deeper. A feeling. Unlike many groups, the best athletes emanate grounded, composed, camaraderie. *Presence.* On the thought alone, my stomach softens, so I stand on tiptoe, and I kiss Lance. "Thank you."

With that kiss, the show launches. Happy, I dance with the guys, under Lance's watch. A guardian. A goalie. A kindhearted man, who complements me, as demonstrated by his mindreading—on the first notes of my favorite song, before I can ask, he sits me on his shoulders.

K. E. GREGG

Well over seven feet up, I appreciate waves of fans, in this oasis, surrounded by twinkling city lights. Overjoyed, I sway to Two Door Cinema Club, "Something Good Can Work."

On the chorus, Lance squeezes my legs. He's connecting the song to my situation.

"Yes," I answer, automatically. Then, I look to the sky; I bask in goodness.

When the music dies, he lowers me to the grass. Shirtless, he pulls the tank from his pocket, dressing to depart. Exchanging hugs, the others break away. In their wake, Lance offers his arm, ever the party gentleman. Outside the festival, he escorts me to late-night food, currywurst, a German dish of pork sausage, curry ketchup, fries. Seated on Lance's lap, I lick my fingers, satisfied. Presenting a napkin, he looks me up and down. "I like you like this."

"Dirty?" I ask, shaking sand from my hair.

"Nah," he insists. "Natural."

17

MAGIC HOUR.

On the cliffs, we walk from Bondi to Coogee and back again, as we have, many evenings. Now, it's my last day in Sydney, so we take our time, strolling, wandering. Along the return, we enter Waverly Cemetery. Among the graves, I consider the utterance that cemeteries are among the richest places on earth, filled with buried treasure—ideas never realized, talents never utilized, passions never pursued.

My body tenses. I stop. "Why water polo?" I ask Lance.

"Because I love it," he says.

"Plus, you're good at it."

"I got good because I love it. I started playing for fun, and I'll play that way for the rest of my life."

I'm taken aback. The sun drapes him in soft light. By his feet, wistful, wilting flowers adorn Henry Lawson's grave. It's a fleeting tribute, among verdant grasses, evincing life's fragility. As my eyes trace the petals, I confess, "I don't have that."

"Yeah, you do," he says.

My face twists in confusion.

"People," he adds.

Quietly, I process his answer. "Come on." He leads me out of the cemetery to a bench facing the ocean. We sit; I place my head on his shoulder; I feel at home. Typically, I would fill the silence, but this time, I hold my tongue.

I wait.

Lance looks outward, observing the horizon. "Grace . . ."

"Yes?"

"You have this way about you, it's positively infectious. When you enjoy something, you *really* enjoy it. And when you light up, everyone lights up."

He pulls my face to look at him. "You love life. You love people. That's your thing."

I nearly start crying. For a young man, he carries an old soul. To the setting sun, he tells me, "I plan on as many Olympics as possible, but if that ever jeopardizes how I feel about water polo, about life, I'll find something else."

"Wouldn't people be devastated?"

"Who cares?"

He's matter-of-fact. Who cares? Yet again, I'm struck.

"Lance?"

"Hey?"

"Now that I'm done with law and politics, think I'll find something else?"

"Of course. What did you dream about as a child?"

"I don't remember."

"You will."

He gives me a kiss. "Come on." We stand; he pulls his iPhone from his pocket, and a few taps later, he christens my future with "Public Service Announcement." Over the cliffs, Jay-Z raps, restoring my power, and invigorated, I dance, shouting to the ocean, "Yes!"

Watching with delight, Lance hugs me off the ground. "There she is."

"Thank you." I kiss him all over. "Thank you."

To nightcap, we visit Lance's local, a surf bar.

At our sight, Hemingway rings the bell. When we hug hello, his long, damp hair smells of hinoki shampoo. Zen.

Cousins turned best friends, Lancelot and Hemingway share epic names, shrugged off by both men. "Our mums like to read." At the bar, Lance asks Hemi, "How were the waves?" Hemi's sun-kissed face foretells his reply, "Great." Hemi's my age, and he used to surf professionally. Most days, he can be found barefoot, heading to or from a break. Otherwise, he's here, serving his community. Hospitable by nature, Hemi rings the bell once more. "What're we drinking?"

"Dealer's choice," Lance says.

"Spirit?" Hemi asks.

"Whiskey," I answer.

Mission-ready, Hemi mixes with mellow mastery. The proof? In his pour. Before serving, he samples his concoction with a pull of a straw. "Tasty." Next, he presents the glasses. "Cheers."

"Great." Lance takes a sip.

"I love it," I agree.

Hemi snaps a piece of chalk. "Shall I add it to the menu? Name it after you?"

"Yes!" I leap from my barstool. As it happened, a namesake cocktail topped my newly minted dream list.

"The Grace?" he asks.

"The Bunny," I say.

"Pardon?" Hemi freezes; Lance swallows laughter.

"It's my alias, for when I want to be wild."

"Who says Grace can't be wild?" Hemi counters.

"My pedigree." I sink into my barstool.

"Ugh." Hemi makes a face, before catching himself. "Sorry, sounds like a drag."

Surf rock plays; I trace the sweat down my glass; Lance rubs my back. "Maybe it's time to own it?" Hemi concurs, "Ye-ah, like be yourself, all the time?" I sit tall. "Imagine." Hemi steps to the chalkboard. "Good, it's sorted."

"What?" I ask.

"You'll leave Bunny in Bondi as a cocktail."

His solution makes me smile. At that, he chalks my fate.

"To Bunny." I raise my cocktail, retiring my double life.

"To Grace Elizabeth McLean," Lance follows.

We drink, then Lance looks at the register. "Hem, is that my *Walden*?"

"Sure is."

"Can I get it back?"

"Perfect timing, finished it this morning."

"Got a pen?"

"Sure thing." Hemi delivers book and pen before stepping away, making himself scarce.

Book in hand, Lance swivels away, shielding his efforts. I stare out at Bondi; I listen to the music, and I hear him write, flip, write, close. Afterward, he swivels back. "A gift."

I hug his *Walden* to my chest. "I've never read it."

"I know." He smiles. "Have a look."

Inside the cover,

1 February 2013—Bondi Beach

May you always be Grace, she's amazing. Also, see page 97.
x Lance

At once, I follow the instruction. On 97, a bracketed passage:

"I went to the woods because I wished to live deliberately, to front only the essential facts of life, and see if I could not learn what it had to teach, and not, when I came to die, discover that I had not lived. I did not wish to live what was not life, living is so dear; nor did I wish to practice resignation, unless it was quite necessary. I wanted to live deep and suck out all the marrow of life . . ."

I rub the passage with my hand, catching Lance's stare. I lower the book; I kiss him profusely. And sealing the deal, he holds my face.

"To the rest of your life."

18

I HUG HIM TIGHTLY.

"Is this good-bye forever?" I ask. He smells of sunscreen.

"Do you want it to be?"

"No."

"Then it's not."

I check my bags; I start away, but I run back, into his arms. As he holds me, I tremble, so he wipes the tears from my eyes. "I'm always here for you."

"Promise?"

"Promise."

"OK."

I clear security; I keep walking; I don't look back.

After takeoff, I lean against the window, as Sydney and romance disappear from view. *What now?* I stare at the clouds, wondering, when sadness comes for me. It's as though leaving Lance permitted sorrow. And blessed by a vacant first class, I cry. It's not sobbing, but releasing—years of sadness, bottled below. I cry tears of faking it and making it, tears of self-betrayal, self-hatred. I cry tears of confusion, separation.

I cry tears of loss.

Then, it passes.

Skipping dinner, I eat ice cream with Valium and wine. Once sedated, I lower my seat to the bed position. Before closing my eyes, I reach for my iPhone. In Lance's contact, I type a note to self:

You resuscitated my heart. For that, I love you.

I stow my phone; I close my eyes; I revisit highlights from my trip. On that, I fall asleep, letting my subconscious weigh the wisdom of Sydney. Many hours later, I land in Los Angeles.

Ready.

19

"RELAX."

I calm myself, on my birthday morning in March. *Relax*, I comfort myself, at a conference table, at Jack's law firm, in Century City. Beside me, Jack, serving as my attorney.

"Freedom?" He hands me a pen.

"Freedom," I answer resolutely, feigning the confidence necessary to continue.

Thirty-two and starting over.

"Alright,"—Jack directs me to the first yellow flag—"it's pretty straight-forward, a lot to sign, but . . . He took care of you."

"Thank you." I squeeze Jack's arm.

"I got you. Remember . . ." he starts.

"This is the beginning," I say.

"Exactly."

And so, over two donuts and a dark roast, Jack guides me page to page, flag to flag. Initial, sign, repeat. Manhattan Beach house, gone. New York apartment, gone. Remaining furniture, gone. Nonprofit, dissolved. Board seats, resigned. Club memberships, gone. Access to boats, gone. Access to jets, gone. Access to cars, gone.

Freedom within reach.

"Last one," Jack tells me, as I stare at the document. A bit nervous, I take a breath, and with shaky strokes, I go from separated to divorced.

"That's it." He hugs me.

"That's it," I echo.

Done.

20

L.A. WOMAN.

I find a West Hollywood bungalow.

Early one morning, my basics arrive from storage. It's strange to watch old items enter a new space. Even so, after months of living on a sofa, this is the right move. It's spring, and off Melrose, garden roses bloom. That evening, a breeze blows through the palms, the jacaranda, the lemon trees, and comforted, I settle in.

On my own.

21

JUNE ARRIVES.

With its gloom.

Chilly, gray weather.

To brighten the haze, I enroll in a ballet class. There, I run into Isla, the wife of my friend Hawk, whom I've known since college. First look, I flush. I've been out of touch with the Duke crew for some time.

"Hey, babe, Hawk told me your news." She hugs me tight.

Her tone settles my nerves. It's entirely kind, caring, which make sense. Her husband, Hawk, is his own man, a bit of a lone wolf. He's always walked his own path, unaffected by the whims of our crew.

After class, she invites me to tea. As we talk, I reveal that I lost most of my friends in the divorce. Rather than commiserate, she finds a silver lining. "You know, Hawk always thought we'd be close. Maybe this is our time."

"I'd like that," I say.

"Did you leave the beach? Do you live up here?"

"I do."

She claps her hands. "May I throw you a dinner?"

"A dinner?"

"With my friends," she offers. "They're incredible women, and they'll adore you."

A smile gives my answer.

"Grace,"—she sips her tea—"don't take this the wrong way, but I'm not worried about you, not at all."

Her confidence inspires my own. It's exactly what I needed to hear.

Belief.

A few weeks later, Isla greets me outside a pop-up restaurant near my neighborhood. Following a rumble of motorcycles, her energetic voice announces, "Girls' night!" She looks stunning, her petite frame in a bodysuit, tucked into trousers. "From Kyoto," she says. We head for the door; she links my arm. "You're going to make a beautiful new life for yourself." Her red lips stretch into a smile. "Let's celebrate."

"I can't wait."

Inside, olive trees twinkle, and the smell of fresh pita fills the room. Awash in sensation, a thought rises, *He'll be here.* My body awakens, but my logic resists, for the prediction makes no sense. *He* was a client, at my former law firm. Last I heard, he moved to Europe. Still, my mind flashes to him. *He'll be here.* For an instant, I want to ask Isla, for he's quite well-known, but . . . I don't.

I let it be.

Soon, we reach a long, candlelit table, strewn with flowers, filled with Isla's friends. From chair to chair, Isla makes my introduction. Hugs, warmth, acceptance. Together, we drink and laugh over small Mediterranean plates. Before dessert, one woman's husband arrives; he's taking her to a concert. Aware of the occasion, he introduces himself. "I'm JD, one of Isla's photographers." I shake his hand; he turns to Isla. "I know her. I've shot her."

As his agent, Isla corrects him. "No, she's a lawyer."

A bit tipsy, I sip my wine. "Former lawyer."

"That's right." Isla clinks my glass.

Processing the information, JD helps his wife, Naomi, with her jacket. Next, Naomi wraps me in a hug. "Welcome to the crew." All the while, JD stands his ground. "I swear I've shot you."

"I don't know what to say." I laugh.

"Well," he concedes, "if we haven't worked together, we will."

They leave for the concert.

"He gets these premonitions." Isla laughs. Then, she hugs me. "Who knows! Anything can happen."

Dessert arrives; I excuse myself for the restroom. Along the way, my mind halts. *He's here.* Convinced, my legs alter their course, mechanically. I head for the entrance, stepping, stepping, until my lips murmur, "There you are."

It's him, the Client, salt and peppered, in a bespoke suit. At close range, I observe him, as admirers swarm and fawn. *Will he remember me?* I start to doubt; I back away, but he looks up.

He waves.

He breaks away from his fans.

He comes to me.

"Grace."

"Hi, how are you?"

"I'm well. You still at the firm?"

"I'm not."

"Back in politics?"

"No."

His eyes widen. "What a mystery."

We laugh.

For a while, we talk, of what I'll never say. In the end, I ask, "You've had tremendous success, what do you envision for me?" The Client's eyes smile; he places his hands in his pockets, which causes his chest to broaden. Standing proud, he tells me, "A giant heart and a lot of love."

My reality bends.

"That sound right?" he asks.

"It does."

"Any other advice?" I ask.

"Smile," he says.

"That's it?"

"That's it."

And flashing his own, he walks away.

Smitten by the encounter, the wisdom, I make it to the restroom. Through the door, I meet a floor-to-ceiling mirror. I pause. Then, facing my reflection, my entire body smiles.

There you are.

22

OCTOBER.

Three months since Isla's dinner. Seven months since divorce.

It's brisk; it's early, and I sit on a terrace, overlooking JD and Naomi's ranch. "Coffee?" Naomi offers, replenishing my mug.

"Thank you."

Gently, the sun spreads through Malibu Canyon. To the light, JD claps his hands. "Almost time." Next, he goes to his studio, where he gathers equipment. In his absence, Naomi rubs my back. "You got this."

"Hope so." I cradle my mug.

"Go time!" JD shouts, so we walk to his blue Ford pickup. When I pile in, he rolls down the window. "Welcome to 1967." Naomi waves both hands. JD taps the leather bench. "F100. Isla says you like cars."

"I do."

"Well then, let's roll." He starts the engine; I buckle up.

Backing out of the drive, butterflies swarm my stomach. Silencing the radio, JD explains, "It's a fine art series on freedom. Think power, escape, rebellion. You know?"

"I do." I take a breath.

"Nice." He cruises up the dirt road to an empty field, surrounded by a wooded expanse. We park; we exit; the field is still dewy. Following JD's lead, I march to the tree line. There, I remove my sheepskin boots, sinking into cold grass. Deep in process, JD decides, "Alright, stay there; I'm crossing over; when I shout run . . . run."

I nod.

"Like you're breaking free. Long, determined strides. Cool?"

"Cool." I present my best poker face, as his Redwing boots crunch away. Alone with my nerves, I stare at passing clouds, seeking solace. Next, I rub my palms together, and like a ballerina in the wings, I tell myself, "*Merde*."

Shit.

Butterflies. Butterflies.

JD shouts, "RUN!" Pushing through fright, I drop my robe. I stand tall. Exposed. I'm chilled, a bit shocked, and yet, I run. Entirely naked, I run. To help, JD cheers, "You look amazing! Keep going!" And so I continue, each stride stronger than the last. Building, sprinting, to the sound of his camera shutter. *Click. Click. Click, click, click, click, click.* No turning back. This is it. No more big law. No more politics.

Done.

My thoughts stop.

I'm lost in the running.

I'm enjoying my freedom.

Done.

On the other side, JD hands me a blanket. "AWESOME." With exhilarated disbelief, I pant under cashmere. For some time, I'd been closing doors. Today, I burn the boat. No retreat. No return. I shake my head; I grin. Soon, I'll be nude in galleries, at shows, for collectors, in books. What a spectacular assurance against backsliding. No more shrinking or hiding. I've stripped all pretense away.

Beside me, JD flips through his memory card. At one point, he zooms in, out, and in again. "Holy shit."

"What?" I ask.

"*Grace*," his voice lowers, "I think we got it." He flashes me the screen. I grow giddy. "I think we did."

Click.

23

"THE LAKERS."

His baritone asserts over voice mail. "Let's go to a game."

It's February 2014.

As promised in Sydney, Vlad has come for me. The night of our date, he knocks at my door, and when I meet him, my lips drift apart—somehow I'd forgotten the power of his presence. Breaking the ice, he kisses my cheeks. "You are more beautiful than I remember."

"Thank you."

At Staples Center, Vlad escorts me to courtside seats. Before sitting, an introduction, someone official-looking.

"Enjoy the game," the man says, excited Vlad is here.

"How do you know him?" I ask.

"I'm a Lakers superfan." Vlad helps me to my seat.

"Are you?" I cross my legs.

"Yes." He sits. "I got to know Kobe in the Olympic Village."

On our left, an agent-type takes notice of the exchange, and asks, "Are you somebody?"

I cringe. Fortunately, Vlad doesn't skip a beat. "No," he answers. "I'm the untalented Gasol brother." I stifle a laugh, and unimpressed, the agent-type turns away.

"Now, we can relax," Vlad whispers. "Want a hot dog?"

"Please."

Hot dogs.

Beer.

Warm-up begins.

"Vlad!" I exclaim, surprised by a player on the opposing team.

"What?"

"I know him!"

"Who?"

"Him! From college!"

"You went to Duke?"

"I did!"

Eighteen again, I wave to my buddy, who laughs and pumps a fist to his chest. Then, I squeeze Vlad's arm. "What a gift."

"My pleasure." He leans into me.

Four quarters later, my Duke friend walks over, bouncing his shoulders, singing Dr. Dre and Snoop Dogg, "Nuthin' But a 'G' Thang."

"B!" I shout.

"G!" he answers.

We reunite.

Worlds collide.

24

POST-GAME.

A new club, in Hollywood. Vlad helps me with my wristband, then we're taken to a back room, to a corner banquette, where B and his teammates hold court. When we arrive, B raises his arms, and Champagne floats in on the wings of cocktail servers with sparklers. Around us, models, bottles, celebrities, and those who follow. Sipping my flute, I hear the DJ spin a memory. "G!" B shouts. Then, he tells Vlad, "This was our song."

"*Was?*" I laugh.

Moments later, we're on the dance floor.

To "The Next Episode," to Dre and Snoop, our feet spark. A dance circle forms.

I'm having the time of my life, until . . . I hit a patch of spilled cocktail. My stilettos slip; I'm Bambi on ice, flailing, flailing, falling.

Boom.

Embarrassed, I look up from the floor. Two couples tower over me, familiar faces. "Hi," I barely choke out the word. It's Finance Guys and Mrs. Finance Guys, friends of my ex-husband. Hopeful, I reach out, but rather than help, they turn their backs.

Burn.

Under the weight of my past, I stay down. Saddened. Stuck. Nearly defeated, I take a breath, when two arms swoop under my shoulders. At once, I'm resurrected, facing B, who hugs me tight. "Red bottoms down!" His joke soothes me with laughter. Relieved, I turn to see who helped. I don't know him, but I recognize him.

He's a famous rapper.

"Thank you." I hold my heart.

"Anytime." His words stretch into mine.

As they do, the music changes; the DJ mixes in my Rap Hero's hit. Hyped, B rolls into the song's dance move. Nonchalantly, my Rap Hero gets involved, beckoning me to join.

So, I dance. We dance. Followed by a group hug.

"Still got it," B says. And as I leave the dance floor, I bless my fall for its outcome. An unbelievable, unforgettable memory.

Back at the banquette, Vlad hugs me. "Brava."

"Apart from the fall," I deflect.

"Do you know the people who turned their backs?" he asks, protective.

"I used to . . ."

"Haters," he states.

"I guess . . ." My voice lowers. Vlad holds me. "We don't hate haters. We *love* them. They're fuel."

"Fact," B says. The guys slap hands, and B adds, "Focus on the people who help, G."

"He's right," Vlad concurs.

"Haters only hurt if you agree with them," B explains. "Do you?"

"No." I'm hesitant.

"What's that?" Vlad gestures for me to level up.

"No." I'm committed.

"Good."

B grabs Champagne, fills my flute. "G, you can't be about everybody. Those who are for you will be with you. It's that easy."

The DJ spins a deep cut.

"That guy's cool, huh?" I look at the booth.

"Very," B says.

"Want to thank him?" Vlad asks.

"I do."

B hails a bouncer to guide me, and I'm off, up, into the booth. Between songs, the DJ hugs me. "We've all been there." His name is Alexander; he's tremendously kind, and we exchange numbers. "Come to a show sometime," he invites.

"I will."

What a night, I reflect, exiting the booth. Far beyond the name game, my people found me. A college friend, an Olympian, a rapper, a DJ. No common bond, but shared values.

Character.

When the lights come on, Vlad takes me home. At my door, he asks, "What do you want?" I fumble for my keys. "I don't know . . ." I look away; I find my keys. Vlad steps closer. "I do." He cocks his head. "I am looking for the love of a lifetime."

My lips float open; my penchant for relationship washes over me. For a second, I'm starry-eyed, then, my priorities prevail. After the divorce, I vowed to stay single, to focus on myself, to balance out a lifetime of serial monogamy. One year since Lance, this represents my longest stretch single since my teens. Enter: Superman. I place my hand on his chest. The temptation is formidable. I'm tingling, pulsing. My inhibitions have been drowned by Champagne. Even so, I tell him, "I'm not ready."

He nods.

His posture straightens. "I understand."

"You do?"

"Of course."

I lift my hand from his chest. He reminds me, "Gold before gold."

Overcome, I pull his face toward mine for a kiss. It goes on and on, until we reach our ending. "Good," he says. "It's bittersweet," I say, as I enter my house. Alone. Before closing the door, I tell him, "You're amazing."

"*You* are," he answers.

"Think I'll be OK?" I ask, suddenly nervous.

"Of course," he insists, tapping his forearm.

"Mind over matter," I remember.

"Good," he concludes.

I blow him a kiss.

He nods.

I close the door.

25

BUZZ.

My iPhone wakes me. *Buzz. Buzz. Buzz.* It falls off the bedside table, still buzzing, onto the flokati rug. Curious, I reach for glowing notifications. B. Isla. Loyal. Even the DJ, Alexander.

Message after message. Love, in response to hate.

Someone leaked my fall to Page Six, no redemption, but thankfully, no photo. Still, gossip traveled fast on social media. In days gone by, my people-pleasing heart would have broken.

Not anymore.

After responding to love, I fluff my pillow; I laugh off the rest, emulating Vlad, "Haters."

Four p.m.

I've slept all day.

Starving, I order pizza.

While waiting, I grow anxious. I pace the house, then I open the linen closet; I remove towels, sheets, napkins, searching for . . . a shoebox. Once I find it, I take it to the bathroom. Inside the shoebox, my secret stash, a Ziplocked holy grail: Percocet, Xanax, Ambien, Adderall, Lunesta, Valium, OxyContin, oh my. Old habits return; I place a Percocet on my tongue; it goes down; I tune out.

Melded to my sofa, I can barely move when there's a knock at the door. Before I can get up, my phone rings, so I tell the delivery man, "It's unlocked, mind coming in?"

He does.

Pajama-clad and hung over, I wait for dinner to be served. At his tentative "Hello," I smooth my silk top. It's a skater boy, with raven, shoulder-length hair. He has soulful eyes, and though he's only eighteen or nineteen, his entrance shifts the room. With composure, he brings my pizza to the sofa. Upon completing the exchange, he nods. "I'll show myself out"; but before going, he tucks his hair behind his ears, and he dares a thought, "I don't know if you know, but you're beautiful."

Startled, I sit upright, admittedly looking my worst. At that, he shakes his head; he points to his chest. "In here."

Now, I'm in my heart, and as if he's aware, he smiles. "Take it easy."

I have no words. The only sound is the scuff of his Vans leaving my house. When the door closes, I throw off my blanket; I march to the bathroom. There, I seize my Ziploc. Straight away, I light candles; I cue music; I place pill bottles on the toilet tank.

Gentle guitar riffs. Heavy guitar riffs. Dave Grohl on drums. To the beat, I sway.

Kurt Cobain fills the room . . . "Smells Like Teen Spirit." I take a breath; I twist open a bottle; the pills rattle. I stop swaying.

I cut myself off.

With a slow tip of my hand, I empty the bottle. Pills splash into the toilet. Around me, music rages. Bottle by bottle, I unleash a cascade of pills into the water. Capsules, discs, mingling, swirling, sinking to grunge rock, as I ping wounded soldiers into my Champagne bucket trash can. A bit dazed, I stare at the blurry mess; I start nodding to the music. Nodding. Bracing. Nodding. Finally, I reach for the handle.

I push it down.

The mess swirls away.

Nirvana.

26

IN THE MAIL, A PACKAGE.

A birthday present from my parents; they're traveling through Italy. It's a case of wine and something gift-wrapped. A book, perhaps. Carefully, I tear open the paper. I'm surprised. It's a leather-bound journal. I've never kept a journal, but in the card, Mom suggests, "For your adventures."

Today, I turn thirty-three. I'm told it's my Jesus year.

For weeks, the gift goes unused, untouched.

March becomes April.

Then, one afternoon, I put pen to paper. On contact, cobalt words rush, gush. It's a feverish, raw, visceral confession. Thoughts, actions, inactions, reactions, all carried, but never admitted. Not even to myself.

By nature, I prefer to stay positive. In so doing, I had ignored my dirty laundry, so much so that it piled to the brink. In this journal, an opening. Permission. I couldn't keep suppressing darkness. If I did, I might burst. And with my little helpers flushed, I had no remedy for implosion.

For that reason, I write.

All month, I write. Not planned, but free. It's real talk. Deep secrets, from the far corners of my soul. Shameful, but necessary. And though pained, I proceed, emptying everything onto unlined pages. My outpouring fills the entire journal. Words upon words.

Spilling.

Slowing.

Stop.

No more shame.

Neither approval nor disapproval, but acceptance.

On instinct, I remove the journal from the cover. I hug it to my chest. Afterward, I store it in a trunk of keepsakes. Out of sight, out of mind. From there, I dress a second journal in my cover. *Will I write again?*

Maybe.

27

MY EYES OPEN.

2012: Honesty.

2013: Leap.

2014: What does it all mean?

On that question, I resume my journaling. Thoughts. Musings. Plus, I read, voraciously: biography, economics, essays, philosophy, psychology, religion, science, more. My happy place is Book Soup in West Hollywood. Armed with titles, I return to my Echo Park routines. In the mornings, I run. My days rotate from cafés to museums to parks to beaches, where I put my legal brain to task, in search of meaning. Isla calls it my PhD in life. A vast, independent study. Supportive, she lets me be, intervening from time to time, with phone calls, study breaks. Some chill. Some wild.

This time, a benefit.

One evening, she calls with an idea, a way to support a cause I adore—UNICEF. "Babe, what if my photographers donate portraits for a silent auction?"

"That'd be wonderful." My perspective zooms beyond myself to the bigger picture. While I had the luxury of contemplation, children were on the run. Refugees. "Let's do it," I say.

And so, we call in favors.

We launch an event.

On the big night, at a house in the hills, our party warms; L.A. sparkles.

There are candles, flowers, desserts, a funk band. "What a turnout," Isla says, as we stroll the silent auction, on our way to check in with a new friend, a dear friend, Wallace. Wallace is a producer, who graciously offered to chair the auction. With iPad in hand, she greets us with hugs, wearing a low-backed dress.

"Ladies, we've already reached our goal," she says.

"So soon?" Isla asks. "How?"

"It's anonymous," Wallace says.

"Anonymous?" I ask.

"There's an anonymous bidder," Wallace explains. "This person asked me to outbid every item for the first hour, which accelerated everything." On her words, unconsciously, her eyes dart to the back bar.

We follow her gaze.

"No!" Isla gasps.

Caught, Wallace whispers, "It's not *not* him."

"I'm going over," I say.

Isla stomps a Louboutin, concerned, for Anonymous was a bad boy, a handsome hound of a musician. "We got eyes on you," Wallace says, pointing two fingers at her long lashes.

"Thank you." I laugh. I turn. I walk over.

Suddenly anxious, I cool myself with a decision, *Forget the rumors, forget the hype, allow this man to introduce himself.*

"Hi." I reach the bar.

"Great party," he engages. It's civil, then he comes on strong, almost— Pavlovian. Rather than cringe, I keep my thoughts on his generosity. "You're Anonymous," I say.

He looks down.

He's off his game.

He looks up. "Wouldn't be if I claimed it."

I pause. I place my hand on his arm. "Well, just in case, *thank you.*"

"Is this your party?" he asks.

"I helped plan it," I say, "and I appreciate you being here."

"Important cause," he says. "Drink?"

"Japanese whiskey."

"Same." He's surprised.

He orders.

We connect.

I move beyond his anonymity. Once served, the Bad Boy tips our bartender, a hundred dollars on an open bar. "Keep drumming," the Bad Boy says. "I will," the bartender answers, raising his chest. Observing the exchange, I sip my drink. Its smokiness warms my throat, as I think out loud, "You're a good man."

Rather than reply, the Bad Boy clinks my glass. Chemistry mounts. Organically. Unlike before, he's off script, and sip by sip, the Bad Boy drops his mask, his mannerisms, his machismo. When he does, I meet the person behind his persona. Meanwhile, the night raises funds beyond expectation. After the total is announced, the Bad Boy asks for my number. I oblige; he sneaks out; the crowd clears.

Pleased, I rejoin Isla, Wallace. We kick off our shoes; we sit with our feet in the hot tub.

"Success."

From success, flirtation.

All summer long with my Bad Boy.

A drink here, a bite there, witty banter, heated stares. It's a game of cat and mouse, without winner or agenda. Rather than race to bedroom or chapel, we practice seduction, for the thrill of it. Our bond defies convention, confounding onlookers. In a way, that heightens our attraction, climaxing . . .

One Hollywood night, at Dan Tana's.

After pasta with Wallace, I have a feeling. I look to the door; my Bad Boy walks in. I smile; he waves; he brings his bassist to say hello. I can tell the bassist has a thing for Wallace, so I invite the guys to join our red leather booth. Around a checkered tablecloth, it's Bad Boy, me, Wallace, bassist. Within minutes, the bassist finds Wallace's hot spot; they gush over movie soundtracks. As for me, my Bad Boy has bad news. "This is my last night in town. We're heading out on tour."

"Oh," I say.

"Will you forget me?" he asks.

"I don't know."

"How can I stand out from your suitors?"

"Well"—my dream list dings—"you do sing. Make it count."

"Will do." He slaps the table.

"What?"

"I'll serenade you." He looks determined. "Give me a sec?"

"Deal."

I ask Wallace to the restroom. Inside, I share, "He's going to sing for me." She nearly drops her clutch. "Here? In front of everyone?"

"We'll see."

"That would be out of character."

"We'll see."

I apply a nude lip. We exit the restroom; I stiletto my return. At our booth, my Bad Boy stands to let me in. As he does, he smiles wide. "I forgot you were wearing leather shorts."

"Oh yeah?"

"They're perfect."

I sit; he sits. My body tingles, anticipation, only . . . he doesn't sing. Wallace shrugs; conversation resumes. A bit deflated, I order a dirty martini; I let go. Once I do, my Bad Boy brushes my hair back.

"Picture us as lovers. Hot. Passionate. Crazy. We spin into a fight. It's messy. We go our separate ways. Time passes, but I can't shake you. I start writing. Letters. I hear nothing. More letters. I reach you. We write back and forth. For months. Then, your letters stop. You vanish. All I have is your words, which I read and reread, alone, by the fire, on my ranch. Missing you."

He leans closer, and in the middle of Dan Tana's, he speaks into song. A sultry cover.

"Legs."

Wallace gasps. The song mounts. Neighboring tables turn. And by the end, you could hear a pin drop. "ZZ Top," my Bad Boy finishes. "I sang it in the past tense . . . for the one who got away."

"Well done." I fall into his arms.

"You like?"

"I like."

He has this clean, classic smell, which I inhale for memory. My Bad Boy proved to be a good man. And more.

A romantic.

28

LABOR DAY WEEKEND.

A staycation. Chateau Marmont. The celebration: lingerie. Isla's new company, a passion project by women for women. In an iconic poolside bungalow, Wallace produces the inaugural photo shoot. I model. Our soundtrack: rock and roll.

After we wrap, we dress for dinner. As night falls, I'm twirling Bolognese beneath bistro lights, my bare legs crossed in a woven chair.

"To friends," Isla toasts.

"A dream weekend," Wallace adds.

"I can't believe this is real life." I raise my glass.

"Cheers."

Our plates clear; I take a moment of appreciation, honesty. "I used to fear my sexiness," I say. "For the way it made women treat me."

"I hear you," Wallace says.

"That's why I make lingerie." Isla takes my hand. "To change the narrative. We're not in competition. My sexy doesn't rob your sexy. It's about femininity, confidence, the joy of being a woman. Every woman deserves to feel her sexiest. Whatever that means to her."

"*Thank you.*" I arch my shoulders, liberated. "Somewhere, I internalized that a woman could be smart *or* sexy. If I played the smart girl, fine. But if I added sexy, I would be shamed: 'What are you doing? What is this? Don't you know how smart you are?'"

"How provincial," Wallace says. "Apologies," she catches herself. "So many of us were programmed that way. It's a vestige of the patriarchy: one power per woman, please."

"Right? Men get to have it all." I shake my head. "Why can't we?"

"We can," Isla intervenes. "We are. And today, we did."

"We did." I recall posing in a balconette bra with my copy of *The Second Sex*. "'The free woman is just being born,'" I quote the author, Simone de Beauvoir.

"What a line." Wallace sighs. "We *can* have it all, and more."

"Day by day." Isla smiles. "With self-love. The more we love and accept ourselves, the more we love and accept each other. If it feels right, that's what matters. Nobody else has to get on board. Each of our truths is our own."

"Well said." Wallace raises her glass.

We toast to women.

Our table is radiant.

"Cheers."

After the check, a nightcap.

Arms linked, we float through arches to the hotel bar. A thought descends, *Heaven*. Soon, Wallace attempts a whisper, "Grace, is that . . . ?" To her question, my eyes sprint, then halt, at a veritable rock god, reclining, royally, in a winged armchair.

"Yes," I say.

"We've been playing his music all weekend!" Isla whispers.

"Your Bad Boy loves him," Wallace notes.

"Same," I say.

"What's the plan?" Isla asks.

"Plan?" I waver.

"This is a sign," Wallace insists. Next, Isla squeezes my arm. "And we're seizing it."

I'm whisked to the Rock God.

When we arrive, Isla is charming, then she and Wallace back away, leaving me . . . presented. "This is Grace," Isla's voice exits.

One Mississippi. Two Mississippi.

Time stretches; the Rock God stands from his chair.

Three Mississippi. Four Mississippi.

"Lovely to meet you, Grace," he says.

I'm awash in his velvety voice. I can't hide my emotions, so I smile and extend my hand. He takes my hand; he kisses my hand. As he does, I see through the scarves, the jewelry, the guy-liner. I see a kindred spirit.

"Hello," I say.

"Hello." He nods.

No longer starstruck, I settle into sweetness. This Rock God is but a man. And from our conversation, he concludes, "You're quite kind, aren't you?"

"I am."

He rubs his jaw. "Stay kind, but stay true."

I nod, then I share, "This is surreal. I've been listening to your music all weekend . . . now, here you are."

"That's life." He laughs.

"Is it?" I beam.

"Yes, love. Perhaps that's my message for you." He looks far into my eyes. "Grace, there are no coincidences. Life is looking out for you."

I take a breath; his words resonate. He looks up.

"There's a place where we're all connected. I get my music there," he says.

His words give me chills.

"If you quiet the noise, you'll find that place. You'll be supported in your truth."

"Thank you," I say, with awareness.

"Enjoy the dance, love." He rocks back, forth.

We smile.

We part.

A few breaths.

I find Wallace and Isla at the bar.

"So?" Wallace asks.

"Better than . . ." I stop, with a splash. A drink spills down my back. Wide-eyed, Isla nudges me to look, while Wallace seeks soda water, a towel. Shaking my dress, I turn to the sound of profuse apologies.

The accent, French. The man, striking, one thousand percent my type.

"My God," he says. "I'm *so* sorry," he apologizes, as Wallace restores me with soda water and towel. "What's your name, sir?" she asks.

"Maxime," he says.

"Maxime, you've just soaked my dear friend Grace. How will you make it up to her?"

Maxime looks at me. He smiles. I smile.

Our connection is instant.

29

CUT TO: MYKONOS.

Summer 2015.

The final destination on a European tour—London, Paris, Berlin, Bordeaux, San Sebastián, Barcelona, Athens. Now, Mykonos. 300 days since Chateau. 300 days, besotted and counting. Why? The man who spilled his drink, a retired French footballer, Maxime Paix. In English, "Greatest Peace." And that's how he affects me, passion with peace. His legacy. As a player, he gained fame as a six, soccer's defensive midfielder. When watching highlights, I notice how he grounded his team, how he moved ahead of plays, opponents, time. Simply put, he flowed, and to his flow, fans chanted.

Maxi Maxi Maxi

Paix Paix Paix

Imagine, thousands of people, chanting for peace. Incredibly, it never went to his head, only his heart. "*Grâce à Dieu,*" he thanked his higher power, with profound faith. After soccer, he traveled the world, transitioning from sports to hospitality. Along his travels, me. And so ended my walk alone. By chance, I gained company.

A lover.

With Maxime came a fascinating crowd: athletes, team owners, hoteliers, restaurateurs, artists, investors, heirs. Over dinners, over drinks, I found myself discussing their many, varied passions. From time to time, I freelanced, using my talents to amplify their efforts. Case by case, I'd contribute writing, fundraising, legal. On the fly, I learned what needed to be done. In short, I used the benefits of my education to collaborate. Maxime nicknamed me *Libera*, Italian for "free," a nod to the old-school *libero*, a soccer position marked by versatility.

My barometer: if you enrich lives, if you serve your community, I'm in. All the way in, to Mykonos.

A house atop a hill with sprawling white architecture draped in bougainvillea. On the property, olive trees, fresh herbs, hammocks, a wine cellar, and an infinity pool merging sky with sea. For us, an ideal summer. The air. The sun. The breeze. Big, bright days. Watercolor sunsets. Starlit nights.

Wash. Rinse. Repeat.

On Mykonos time, my routines take a new tempo. Sleeping in, jogging cloud-kissed roads, breakfasts poolside, coffee in town, secluded beaches, lazy lunches, afternoon delight, naps, dinners, live music, dancing, late-night pleasure…often until dawn. Effortlessly, I embrace the rhythm, heavenly not hedonistic, as intimate as unforgettable.

In French, *joie de vivre*.

In Greek, *meraki*, the pouring of one's soul into everything.

One day, before lunch, we tan at our favorite beach on a navy-cushioned double chaise. Beside me, Maxime stretches his 6'3" frame, decorated by bright, Vilebrequin trunks. To beat the heat, he sprays me with Evian.

From my bag, I reach for *L'Étranger*.

"Albert Camus?" Maxime asks.

"Yes, I love the way he writes."

"And the story?"

"That life is absurd? Not sure I agree."

"I like it." He kisses my shoulder. "To me, if life is absurd, if life has no meaning, we get to make one."

My perspective shifts.

Maxime taps my leg, suggesting a swim. In turquoise waters, I float on my back, staring at rugged terrain. Alone with my thoughts, I consider meaning. *Was Maxi right? After all this searching, was it up to me? If so, what to choose?* Floating. Floating. *Joy.* The word soothes me. *Joy.* I break my float; I submerge. When I return for air, I watch Maxime swim laps, meditatively. His freestyle takes me to Sydney, to Lance. "You love life."

I do.

Meraki.

Giddy, I swim to shore; Maxime follows. As I race up hot sand, he chases me; he catches me; he honeymoon-carries me to our chaise. Together, we air dry, and I stop reading to survey my surroundings. Mykonos. Greece. Earth. If I landed here, amid pristine Mediterranean beauty, I would be convinced that the purpose of this planet is paradise.

"Hungry?" Maxime asks.

"Yes." I roll into him.

"Let's lunch."

He stands; he dresses; my eyes travel his body. Across his heart, a tattoo, typewritten, as if he came with small print, *Vivez Sans Regrets*. "*Ela, Libera*," he nudges me, throwing on a T-shirt. "Yes, sir." I button my jean cutoffs; I add a white linen top. Next, he hands me a motorcycle helmet, and playfully he slaps my ass. "*On y va!*"

By Triumph, we reach a table for two overlooking Delos, the island of Apollo. I nuzzle into Maxime; we talk mythology. And though the island is at a distance, I am magnetized. "*Kalimera*." A man visits our table. Visibly, he's a fan. Maxime started his career in Athens, so he's fluent in Greek, and to this day, fans approach him. Celebrate him.

For my benefit, they switch to English. This fan is the restaurant's owner, so Maxime orders a feast, paired with white wine. "A *Greek* wine," the owner insists.

Over that wine, Maxime and I share fresh-baked pita, olives, hummus, grilled octopus, tomato and cucumber salad, fried truffle potatoes, lamb, and flaming saganaki cheese. Time lazes by, and I can't imagine dessert, but Maxime insists, "*Loukoumades*."

Quite formal, the plate arrives, topped by a silver dome.

"*Ela*, Grace." He nods. "Open your treat."

When I remove the lid, there's a decadent surprise. Honey dumplings encircling an ivory box.

"What?" I ask.

"You don't wear a watch," he says.

"No." I think of the two I sold to start over.

"Time is precious." He kisses me.

I take a bite of the *loukoumades*, which gets a rise out of him. He pulls me into his arms; he softly bites my neck. "Open."

I lift the crown-embossed lid.

Underneath, there's a forest green case, gold stamped: ROLEX SA – GENEVE SUISSE. I remove the case from its box; I take a breath; I open.

"Maxi." My eyes are teary.

Elegant. Understated. Me. An Oyster Perpetual with a navy blue face. Touched, I remove his thoughtful gesture. As I do, he guides my hands to the back, to an engraved message:

Vivez Sans Regrets.

Overcome, I set down the watch; I pull Maxime's face into my hands. I kiss him; he kisses me. I'm hot, flushed, seen. Like that, I press my forehead to Maxime's, no words, when I hear a man clearing his throat.

"Maxime." The man nears the table.

"Yiannis!" Maxime stands; he pulls out a chair. "Come, sit."

Ever-accommodating, Maxime introduces me to his watch dealer.

"I'm here to size your watch," Yiannis says.

I turn to Maxime. "How thoughtful of you."

"He's a keeper," Yiannis says, then he sits to commence his work. While sizing, he talks with us. Greek history. Greek culture. And nearly finished, he asks, "Do you know what Yiannis means?"

"I don't," I say.

He asks for my wrist.

He slides on my gift.

He fastens the clasp.

"God is gracious."

30

EARLY MORNING, ATHENS.

Back from Mykonos, we scale ancient steps. Higher. Higher.

During the walk, no words seem appropriate. Or even, necessary. At the summit, a distressed Greek flag flaps in the wind. Slowly, we circle the ruins, rounding the Parthenon.

"Maxi, my God," I say, gazing up at columns. I have this strange sense of homecoming, *Have I been here before?* The sensation intensifies. A spiraling, up my spine. I rub my arms; Maxime holds me. "*C'est cool, non?*"

"Beyond." I sigh.

Time passes; Maxime taps my watch. "Let's charge it."

"What?"

"I'll show you," he says. "I did this in the beginning of my career. I do it every time I visit."

He takes off his Omega. He holds it in his hand, explaining, "Think of something you want; set the intention; let your watch hold the intention."

I remove my watch; I kiss it; I hold it in my hands, which I pull to my heart. *Joy*, I decide. *May every day bring joy.* With that, my Rolex becomes my talisman.

"All set?" Maxime asks.

"Yes," I say.

"*Brava.*" He kisses the top of my head. We refasten our watches.

Hand in hand, we descend the Acropolis steps; back to town, back to our hotel, back to bed.

"Happy?" he asks, so I show him. "Very."

We have supercharged sex, again and again. Room service comes, goes. I'm ecstatic. I'm calm. I'm tangled in his body, our sheets. He's breathless. My skin glistens. We crave nothing. We're turned on by everything. The bed does its job.

And we stay there all day.

31

MY FEET CLACK AGAINST COBBLESTONE.

Athens is quiet, apart from the occasional passerby.

"*Eh!*"

"*Yia sou!*"

"*Bravo!*"

And other cheers, lost in translation. Kindly, Maxime nods to each and every fan. In between, he pulls me close, renewing his affection. One block, we're walking on confetti. "A party," Maxime says. Next, we reach an alley, torches, a dining club. At the callbox, he enters a code; the door opens. Welcomed warmly, we wind up a circular staircase, passing a bar, a lounge, a gallery, up to the maître d', who kisses our cheeks and seats us at a corner table. "Maxime's table," he says.

It's chilly for September, and a fire is burning. Shadows dance up the wall, and we prepare for haute-Greek. Course by course, Maxime describes our meal in delicious detail. He's an incorrigible giver, and he wants me to love Athens, as he does. "It tastes better with you beside me." He feeds me our last bite.

"*Je t'aime . . . agapi mou.*"

I love you . . . my love.

In French. In Greek.

I love you, my love.

After espresso, Maxime's car awaits. The Aston Martin V12 Vanquish. Tonight, Maxime trades drinking for another pleasure. Driving.

"I have a surprise." He sits me in the passenger seat. Immensely attracted, I buckle up. As he takes the wheel, the Egyptian ankh on his forearm bulges. "Ready?"

"Yes."

We take off.

A paramount driver, Maxime races out of Athens. He's excited, but precise. His command allows me to relinquish control. By now, I trust him to keep me safe, protected. Staring out the window, I'm enchanted. I let go. Overhead, cool air floods the panoramic sunroof, as my seat hugs me, and I trace my fingers up the quilted leather. The farther we drive, the clearer the stars. On the stereo, Johnny Hallyday, covering Jimi Hendrix.

It's "Hey Joe," in French.

I raise the volume.

I'm bathed in rock and roll, when we pull up to a warehouse. "*Bouzoukia,*" Maxime says.

Out of the car, bouncers usher us into debauchery, passing hundreds of guests, en route to a table, framing the stage. At the table, Maxime's friends leap to greet us, surrounded by platters of fruit and flowers. Amazed, I take my seat, and Maxime drapes his arm around me. "Here we go."

I laugh, so he elaborates. "If you like a singer, throw flowers. You can throw and throw as much as you like." I reach for a white blossom; I play with it in my hand. Maxime brushes my cheek. "You will love it."

The lights drop.

Showtime.

First, a red spotlight. In its beam, a tall woman, wearing a glittering gown slit to her waist. Anguished, she sings a sad, suffering song. Strutting the stage, she makes her way to our table; she bows to Maxime. Moved, I fill my hands with flowers, as Maxime whispers, "*Ela.*"

I stand from my seat, and I praise the singer with flowers. On my mark, the crowd erupts, a blizzard of pink, red, white petals. It's sublime. Spectacular.

Maxime's right; I love it.

Her show goes on, and when she finishes, attendants sweep the stage, resetting drama. Next, a blue light, for the headliner, a renowned male singer. His appearance commands shrieks and shouts from every woman in the audience. Ardently, the femme-Greeks clap their hands, as they stand on chairs. Aware of Maxime's repute, I defer to him. "OK if I dance?"

"*Non*," he says, quite firm, quite unlike him.

"OK." I understand, content to admire others.

"*Non*," he repeats, "for you, the stage."

I slap his chest. He's joking. He waves over the singer; his friends clear a path on the table. He's not joking. "*Ela.*" Maxime stands; a new spotlight hits us. Activated, I let him help me onto the table. He slaps my ass; I strut from audience to stage to the singer. I can't understand a word, but I know what to do.

Dance.

At first, slow. Then, I gain power. The star takes notice. We're firing, when I recognize the music; it's a cover of a song by Antonis Remos, a song that Maxime adores.

"*Pia Nomizis Pos Ise.*"

Down below, Maxime fills his hands, singing along. We lock eyes; we smile; he showers me in fistfuls of flowers. Behind him, a waiter with a stack of platters. For the entire song, Maxime throws flowers. His friends throw flowers. The crowd throws flowers. And flowers.

Mesmerized, I twirl under petals. And when the song finishes, the flowers have piled knee-high. Impassioned, the singer dips me backward. Our bow. Upside down, I spot Maxime, clapping, laughing.

I've never seen him look happier.

From the stage, Maxime lowers me back to our table, back to his arms. Music. Flowers. Music. Flowers. The lights come on. I'm sweaty. I'm over the moon. We hug our good-byes and drive back to the city's center. Starving, I make eyes at Maxime.

"Souvlaki." He smiles.

With his arm around me, we wander between night and day. After ordering from his secret spot, we find a bench beneath the illuminated

Acropolis. Nearby, a lone violin plays Bach, as I eat fresh carved pork with tzatziki wrapped in grilled pita. To the music, I ask Maxime, "What does *ela* mean?"

"Finally, she asks," he jokes. Then, he kisses my forehead. "I use it for fun. To me, it means, come on, enjoy life."

"*Ela*." I cherish the word. I've never felt happier.

This, I tell myself.

Always remember this.

32

FALL, WINTER.

Back in L.A.: projects, passion, enjoyment.

2016.

All the while, Maxime has commuted between Europe and L.A. On the stroke of March, we plan to meet in New York. At LAX, I board my plane. I find my seat. I hear my name.

"G!"

"B!" I leap to hug my dear friend. It's been a while. "Aren't you in season?" I ask.

"Nah,"—he taps his knee—"game over."

"I'm so sorry." I hug him again. "I hadn't heard."

"All good. Now, we get to pick a new city."

"Is your wife happy?"

"Thrilled."

"L.A.? New York?"

"Maybe." He laughs.

Crossing the country, we catch up. When asked, I rave about my man, travel, helping dreamers with dreams.

"Cool, cool," B supports me, before prodding, "What about your dream?"

I bite my lip, stumped. His inquiry reveals a blind spot. I'd been dreaming . . . vicariously. "Drink?" the flight attendant offers, rescuing me. I ask for sparkling water; B lets the point go; we return to laughter.

Through JFK, we make our way to the baggage claim. At the carousel, B helps me with my suitcase, which I hand to my driver. "Always good to see you." B hugs me.

"You too," I say; he lets go.

"G, I've got nothing but love for you."

"But?" I sense a *but*.

"You deserve your own dream."

My heart accelerates. B has touched a truth.

"For what it's worth,"—he smiles—"I think helping others is helping you."

"Find my dream?"

"Yep." He nods.

"I hope so." I squeeze his arm. And as I walk away, I hear him shout encouragement.

"Get that dream, G. Get it!"

33

STEAM FILLS THE BATHROOM.

In the shower, hot water rushes down, casting me in a cloud of Le Labo Rose 31. B's words replay in my mind, *Get that dream*. A bit anxious, I shampoo. No reprieve. I condition. His call-out stays with me. *Get that dream*. I bite my lip. My nerves percolate, and out of nowhere, I shout, "WHAT DREAM?"

I'm startled, but I repeat my demand, "WHAT DREAM?" I'm desperate, shouting to whomever, whatever might be listening. My vocal cords throb; my fists are clenched; and soon, rage forces tears from my eyes.

I collapse to the shower floor. Sobbing. "I'm trying, I'M TRYING," I plead. "What more do you want? If you're out there, if you fucking care, HELP ME." I release a guttural scream. It's ghastly; it echoes off the shower stall. I'm sobbing, sobbing. The pain pierces, peaks, crashes.

The pain subsides. My tears halt.

My body relaxes. I return to standing. No resolution, but a sense of release, recovery. I rinse off. As I do, a voice descends upon me, filling me, my mind, my being with calm.

Three words, repeating.

Tout va bien.

Tout va bien.

Tout va bien.

All is well.

My inner voice connects with something higher, something the Rock God described, way back when, at Chateau. Now, I understand, and I'm comforted by his introduction. Increasingly soothed, I end my shower; I step onto a plush mat; I towel dry. Then, in a dazed but tranquil state, I massage in body lotion; I dress in the hotel robe. Out of the bathroom, into the suite, I collapse upon the bed. Two hours until Maxime. I close my eyes; a knock at the door. Uninterested, I feign absence, but the knock persists. "It's the manager. I have something for you."

Reluctant, I answer to find a well-tailored Frenchman with a bucket of Champagne. "Compliments of the hotel," he says. My hand covers my heart. "How lovely."

"May I come in?"

"Please."

Near the window, overlooking twilight Manhattan, he pops the bottle and fills a coupe. Adjusting my robe, I accept his gift, only my arm trembles, and the bubbles spill. I hop back, embarrassed, but before I can apologize, he refills my glass. "*Tout va bien.*" He shakes his head, confused by his use of French, "Excuse me, I meant, all is well."

Mystified, I raise my glass. He smiles; his phone rings, so he asks, "Do you need anything else?"

"No, thank you," I say.

"Take care," he says into my eyes.

He leaves.

Sipping my gift, I stare at New York. *What a day.* Then, for the first time since childhood, I approach the bed; I get on my knees in prayer. Entirely vulnerable, I thank whomever, whatever might be listening. If there were ever a way to get my attention, Champagne. During my prayer, I gain insight. Instead of panicking or pleading, I can listen. I can pay attention. To moments before me. To guidance from others. To guidance from myself. To life, looking out for me.

"Thank you," I say aloud, as I return to standing.

Tout va bien.

34

A CHILL.

On my birthday eve, the city freezes. Despite the cold, Maxime dares me to dress up, so I wear stilettos, thigh-high stockings, and a silk minidress beneath a family fur, the one passed down from my great-grandmother. On its silk lining, her initials, my grandmother's initials, my initials.

Past a neon "Rare Books" sign, Maxime rushes me in from the cold, taking my fur, allowing me to make my entrance into our friend's speakeasy. Coming our way, I spot a towering, Bic-shaven head.

"Miro!" I hug him.

"Welcome." He hugs me; he hugs Maxime; he places his hands together, a genuine showing of namaste.

Around us, the space is aglow, lamplight, candles, doubled by a mirrored wall of spirits. Tending the wall, experts in white jackets mix drinks to Blondie. "Rapture." Back in the back, Miro seats us at a table, for dinner. On his command, two Manhattans arrive, which Miro offers with a toast, "More life."

While sipping the specialty, Maxime and I take in the scene. "Feel the energy," Maxime says.

"It's magic," I agree.

Post-aperitif, dinner is served, orchestrated by the chef. There's table-side steak tartare, fish, pasta, chocolate, cheese. My senses are heightened. It's magnificent. Punk rock plays. Silverware clinks. Maxime asks, "What do you want for thirty-five?"

"More guidance on my path," I say.

The check arrives; Maxime opens the leather holder and laughs, flashing me the total. In place of charges, a handwritten note, "Happy birthday, Grace."

I rush to the bar; I kiss Miro's cheek; I beg him to join us. "Be right there," he says. Moments later, he's beside me, with ingredients for custom after-dinner drinks. As he mixes, I wonder, "What makes a good bartender?"

"Acceptance."

"Interesting." Maxime nods. Miro goes on, "He welcomes you. He never judges you. He embraces you as you are. If you feel accepted . . . you're in the presence of greatness."

My shoulders drop.

"To Grace." He presents our drinks. "Your name suits you."

"To Miro," I reply. "What does Miro mean?"

"It comes from *miru*." He nods. "Peace."

"You're surrounded," Maxime jokes.

We drink.

Outside the speakeasy, a car from our hotel. Cozied in the backseat, I lay my head on Maxime's shoulder. "Bed?"

"Nightcap?" he suggests.

"OK."

"*On y va.*" He kisses my head. "To Soho," he instructs the driver.

When we arrive, I exit the car. "It's snowing!" Like a little girl, I raise my face to the flurries. Light, ethereal snowfall. Charmed, Maxime wraps himself around me. "Let's get you inside."

Like that, he ushers me into our destination: Cipriani. Inside, I shake out my hair, as the room calls out, "Surprise!"

A birthday party, with Isla, Hawk. Wallace, her new boyfriend, Dean. Jack. Mom and Dad. Loyal, his girlfriend, Dechen. L.A. friends. New York friends. European friends. Finally, B and his wife.

"How'd I do?" B laughs.

"Crushed it," I say. "I had no clue."

Hugs follow hugs, leading to midnight.

The music stops.

The music changes.

A riff.

A beat.

"Paradise City."

The kitchen doors swing open, revealing Cipriani's signature vanilla meringue. The cake moves toward me with sparklers, candles, and everyone singing Guns N' Roses.

I'm dancing; I'm floating; the cake reaches me.

Faced with a wish, I listen, as one year turns to another. In the stillness, a thought descends. My wish. With confidence, I pull back my hair; I take a breath; I extinguish my candles.

Peace.

35

TIBETAN PRAYER FLAGS LINE THE ENTRY.

The smell of espresso. A hint of chocolate. Neighbors congregate around a matte black Marzocco. Maxime had a meeting, so I reunite with the DJ who saved me from dance floor disaster. Alexander. He's in town for a layover, so he suggests, "Coffee?"

Together, we order. While waiting, I admire the appliqués on his bomber jacket. Roses. A dove of peace. We receive our drinks. Mine comes with a handwritten napkin.

"What's this?" I ask the barista. Through a well-groomed beard, he explains, "One of our regulars is a poet. Whenever he comes in, I ask him to write on our napkins."

"Have a read." Alexander nudges me.

Inhale possibility
Exhale simplicity

The missive pulls me from head to heart. For safekeeping, I fold the napkin into my Moncler pocket. Then, I sit with Alexander. Without discussion, we skip small talk for topics that water the soul. At one point, the coffee shop door jingles. Its bells introduce a vision, a young man in a navy pea coat, collar up, as if to frame a sensitive soul.

"Baby Bob Dylan," I say to Alexander.

"That's the poet," he says. I brighten, *Baby Bob Dylan indeed.* Alexander waves him over, and then there were three. Fast friends, we click. Morning builds to noon; Alexander has to fly. Necker Island. We hug, then the poet asks me, "Grace, care to walk?"

"That'd be lovely."

The day is dusted in snow, but the sun is shining, warming New York toward spring. After roaming free, we reach Washington Square Park. I head for the arch, and underneath, I make a request. "Would you share a poem?"

He's shy.

I spread my arms. "What better stage?"

To that, he laughs, and from laughter, poetry. Rhythmic. Existential. Speaking to his life, as it speaks to my own. Face to face, he performs for me, briefly, yet sincerely. When he finishes, he bows his head. A jolt. I'm struck. And when he looks up, I swear he notices.

I shift.

On impulse, we hug. Heart to heart. "Lady Grace." He backs away. "Lady Grace." He waves good-bye.

Uplifted, I stroll back through Greenwich Village. No destination in mind, yet there's this strange inner pull guiding me to a building where I halt. I don't recognize the building; still, I'm drawn to the entry, where I lean against the brick. Twenty, thirty minutes lapse. *I must look crazy*, I think, but I don't care; I lean on.

Comforted.

Eventually, my eyes wander. *Where am I? What is this?* As I survey the scene, I notice a plaque: 93 MacDougal—*Site of the San Remo Café*, hangout for artists, poets, and writers until 1967. Astonished, I place my hand on the words. A few tears warm my cheeks. *This is it.* I smile; I walk on, back to Washington Square Park. Near the center, I sit on a bench, in view of a colorful chalked mandala. Staring into the symbol, I remember. My meaning. My dream.

I am a writer.

36

A PINK SUPERMOON.

April. Over the desert. Over a music festival. Coachella.

Friday night, LCD Soundsystem. Isla, Wallace, me, with artist passes. Seeking tequila, we visit the VIP bar. Soon, Isla's swaying. "Grace, doesn't this . . ." She moves into dance. Right, two, three, clap. Left, two, three, clap. Back, two, three, clap. Forward. Back. She rotates; I'm with her. We rotate; Wallace joins.

"Dance Yrself Clean."

Around us, young Coachellans gather. "Did you make up an LCD dance?"

Isla laughs. "It's the Electric Slide."

Blank stares.

"Come on." Isla waves. "We'll teach you."

More people join. We dance. From strangers to friends, we dance. A group of teens, twenty-somethings, thirty-somethings. Together. Present.

Dancing.

Saturday.

The brightest shade of moon, named pink for abundance. Spring's bloom.

"Babe, are you excited?" Isla asks.

"Beyond." I stare up, the night's wind in my hair.

Wallace and Isla make conversation. My mind flashes to my prep-school courtyard. Age nine. One afternoon, I waited for my ride, pushing down knee socks, pulling out my French braid. Our family's Volvo station wagon arrived, Loyal in the back seat, our Parisian nanny, Sophie, at the wheel.

"Hi." I sulked into the front seat, weighed down by my uniform, my homework, their rules.

"I have a gift for you!" Sophie smiled.

"A gift?" I'm shocked; there was no occasion.

In the remembering, I can smell Sophie's Chanel No. 5. She placed a hand on my shoulder; she handed me a Laura Ashley–wrapped square. With caution, I peeled back the paper, revealing my first CD.

Appetite for Destruction.

Patiently, Sophie helped me remove layered plastic. Then, she placed the disc in the CD changer, cuing her favorite track. Nine. The carpool line honked; Sophie didn't care. Instead, she cranked open the sunroof and raised the volume. "Grace,"—she looked at me, kicking the car into drive—"never let them tame you."

Off we drove, singing through the school gates, "Sweet Child O' Mine."

From that day forward, a bond. Through prep school, college, law school, marriage, divorce—GNR brought liberation. Home alone, driving my car, working out, on a plane, at a party, any time, any place. For my highs, my lows, GNR never failed. A supreme, secret weapon. Resetting my spirit. Rekindling my fire. At times, the world caged me, but it never tamed me. To GNR, I stayed wild.

Shrieks. Shouts. Anticipation.

I snap back to Coachella. Front, stage left, on the grass. I turn around; I buzz with the intensity of a hundred thousand fans. Wallace and Isla flank me. The palm trees sway in purple spotlights. Isla takes my hand.

Hush.

Hush.

BOOM.

The pyrotechnics burst. And against all odds, Guns N' Roses reunites, here, now. My response defies expression, but for reference: Beatlemania. Not the hysteria, the all-encompassing love. A love that kept me wild. Guns N' Fucking Roses.

Teary-eyed, I sing to every song. All the while, Slash, in his top hat, riffs me out of body. At age nine, the band found me. At thirty-five, they're back. Live.

"Thank you." I wrap my arms around Isla. "What a birthday present."

Isla hugs me; Wallace hugs me; Axl takes to the piano, and thunder-storms cover stage-high screens. "November Rain." Electrified, I grow taller. On firm footing, I sway. Entranced. In the movement, my heart, my mind centers on certain lyrics.

A thought flashes, *I need more time alone.*

I look up; Duff plays over on bass, and in this fatherly, fearless way, he makes eye contact; he nods. I place a hand to my heart; he plays away. The right look at the right time. I have no idea why, but it answers my questions. No logic, no explanation, only this sense.

A knowingness.

37

FIFTY MOTORCYCLES.

Revving. Assembled in Hollywood. Headlights on.

I flip my hair forward; I strap on my helmet; my neighbor Moses reminds me, "Watch the pipes." Carefully, I sit behind him, straddling his custom FXR.

"Ready?" he asks.

I squeeze my arms around his waist. "Ready."

"Hold on tight."

He raises a fist to the night, triggering shouts, howls. On the uproar, he taps my hand, a final check before takeoff. Outside his shop, cameras film, as we peel up the sidewalk, onto the road. Following our lead, fifty motorcycles. A joyride. A night ride. A band of outlaws. Family, by choice, by passion, in fierce formation, looking out, taking care, for the love of the ride. Through L.A., we ride it like we stole it.

Reborn free.

At Hollywood Boulevard, police remove barriers, granting access. As we rip by the barricade, I feel Moses laugh.

Past the police, we cruise a gauntlet of bikes, a formidable line-up, this edgy infantry of choppers, racers, cruisers, all parked, perfectly, facing out at attention. It's breathtaking, and if you were new to earth, you'd likely assume—renegades rule.

Near the front, we slow, as a coordinator points us to the step and repeat. Another laugh, Moses hops the curb, and instead of walking, I ride my first red carpet. Cameras flash, cameras film. "Moses! Here!" All the while, I can't contain my smile, so I whisper to Moses, "You can't make me this happy and expect me to hard face the camera." That makes him break character, and I hope the media captures his smile, for Moses is an angel.

After the fuss, another coordinator removes orange cones, and we park at the foot of famed stairs. On the dismount, we remove our helmets; Moses offers his arm. Together, we stride toward the theater. At its door, I'm handed a frosty tallboy in a paper bag. On my first sip, attendants open the theater doors. "Enjoy." At our entrance, the audience stands, clapping, whistling. Forever modest, Moses flips a middle finger, which sends them over the top. Walking the ruckus, we reach the front row, taking our seats among bikers and actors who portray bikers. We sit. Moses introduces me to a heavily pierced, mustachioed man, who offers, "Popcorn?"

Charmed, I accept. Then, the theater darkens; the movie begins.

Over Blue Ribbon beer, we celebrate Moses. On the big screen. From beginning to end, I experience a previously unknown world, his world, as an insider. It touches me. Profoundly. I think, *What would life be like, if we were all described by a lover?* After all, as humans, we're nuanced. Complex. For this reason, we see each other in a myriad of ways. *What if we look for the love?*

At first blush, I sit surrounded by rough, tough riders. On closer review, each and every one has tenderness. Something to be treasured.

Humanity.

When the credits run, I rise in ovation. I'm part of the resounding applause, but Moses sneaks me out a side door, escaping accolades. Moving with purpose, we hop on his bike; we white-line away to a gas station for street tacos. My lips burn with hot sauce, when he asks, "Afterparty or another ride?"

"Let's ride." I reach for my helmet.

"Listen to the Doors," he suggests, so I put in headphones.

Up Sunset, I'm listening to "L.A. Woman," when we turn left. Downhill, Moses's gloved hand points to a property. The Alta Cienega Motel. We veer off; we park; he leads me up dated stairs, past pea-green doors, to Room 32.

"Jim Morrison's room," he says, knocking. Next, he asks the German occupants, "Can we check it out?"

"*Ja*," they welcome us, so we take a five-cent tour of a grimy shrine to the Lizard King. My eyes climb graffitied walls; my Isabel Marant boots crunch seventies carpet. By the bed, I shudder. Not fear, but a pointed presence. It's strange, yet familiar. So familiar that I tighten my jacket; I exit.

"Cool, right?" Moses follows.

"Trippy."

Back in our neighborhood, late night. Moses parks his bike; we enter the party where two riders are dueling with wheelies. Around them, members of Moses's crew sit in groups, warmed by trash can fires. Moses grabs two lawn chairs, two beers. We sit, a bit removed; I crack my beer, and on the *psssht*, Moses asks, "So?"

"Sooo,"—I take a gulp—"awesome." Another gulp, and I survey his crew. "Moses?"

"Yeah?"

"Have you ever spent time alone?"

He lights a joint. He inhales; he exhales; he answers, "I died."

I drop my beer. On the asphalt it glugs, audibly, before I right it. "Died?"

He nods. "Ten years ago, a drunk driver hit me. I skidded, crashed, and at the hospital, I flat-lined. Gone. In the echo, I reviewed life. Only, it wasn't *my* life. Back then, I was fucking off, running through chicks, doing nothing. Grace . . . it was the life of the man I could've been . . ."

I pull my fingers through my hair. "*Moses . . .*"

"Heavy, right?"

I sip my beer. He carries on, "It's tough to describe, but I think I was given a choice. To mail it in, or come back." He claps his hands. "Blackout. I wake up in the ICU." His voice softens; he impersonates his nurse: "Welcome back Moses, you're a lucky man."

Moses takes another hit, he squeezes his right leg. "From there, I got a metal femur, bunch of pins, a shit ton of alone time. All laid up, I had to face myself, my choices, all the times life asked me to step up, all the times I ran." He continues, "Then, the check came. A big-ass settlement. With that, I could become the man I saw."

"Your shop." It clicks.

"My shop." He looks around. "This is all an accident. A shitty, drunk driver's accident." He stretches his legs, left over right. "But I needed it. Death is one hell of a motivator."

"May I?" I get up for a hug. He stomps out his joint with his Vans.

"Sweet Grace . . ." He laughs. "Bring it in."

We hug.

I return to my chair; he sighs. "Grace, my shop is my heaven. Plus, I get to bring my boys along."

I'm speechless.

He cracks his neck. "I don't know what you're getting at, but in my experience, if life makes a request, don't make it yell. Step up."

BAM. Wooooooo. BAM. Woooooooooo.

Fireworks explode, from the far side of the lot. I finish my beer; I stare at the sparks. "Looks like I'm starting over."

I crush my can.

"Again."

38

YOU ARE HERE.

I read a painted heart on a warped mirror. It tells me, *You are here.*

Maxime squeezes my hand on the patio of the Canyon Country Store. Where we stand, back in the day, music played—Frank Zappa, Joni

Mitchell. More. We're just above the Sunset Strip, but it feels like wilderness. Earlier, Maxime shared another Jim Morrison haunt, a bougainvillea-covered house. Nearby, a city sign designates "Love Street," the inspiration for the Doors' song.

It's a warm spring night, and it's quiet in the foothills of Laurel Canyon. The air smells of flowers, eucalyptus. Nearby, a couple blazes, as if cued by Hollywood—marijuana, the scent of boho-heaven. Exchanging smiles, we pass through their smoke, downstairs, to Pace.

Cozy, candlelit, Italian.

"*Pizza e vino,*" Maxime says. Wine opens, and he updates me on Europe, on his latest hotel project. Enthused, I cheer him on, slice after slice. When we finish, I pull remnants from the tray; I eat the last bit of cheese; I wipe my hands with my napkin. Afterward, Maxime takes my hand. "You know, Jim Morrison lived in Paris."

"Yes," I say, at his touch. Our chemistry is as strong as the day we met. He kisses my hand. "Maybe you should too." I tilt my head; he smiles. "Move to Paris. Move in with me."

My cheeks flush. "Paris." I reach for my wine. "A writer's dream," I say, which Maxime takes as a yes. "Perfect." Butterflies fill my stomach. I can't tell if I'm nervous or excited, so I toast his glass.

"Paris."

39

I TOSS; I TURN; I SLEEP.

At sunrise, my eyes pop open. In Maxime's arms, I think about Paris. *I can be alone, with him. I can start over, with him. The best of both worlds.*

Convinced, I sneak out of bed, craving Canter's bagels. I leave a note; I dress, and quietly, I exit the house. Out front, I smell the rose bushes; I admire the classic, Craftsman bungalow. Already nostalgic, I slide into my car. Soon, all of this will change. I start the car, syncing music, but the stereo fritzes. No connection. Confused, I restart the car, jumping at full volume. The Doors.

"Love Street."

A random radio station, blasting. I grab at the dial, rushing for calm. With the music lowered, I listen. Jim Morrison sings of wisdom, of knowing. Love.

"La, la, la, la, la, la, la." I cruise through West Hollywood beneath a canopy of weeping fig and palm trees. A new day glints in sunshine; the world is my own . . . then, an interruption. Last night's dream. I start shaking, so I pull over; I park. Short of breath, I throw open the door. Air. I need air. A bit frantic, I exit the car; I rush around to the curb, where I sit on a patch of grass, my car dinging, my face in my hands.

I'm back in the dream.

It's a foggy beach. I'm with a man, but I can't see his face. Everything's a blur, apart from the diamond waves lapping at our feet. Slowly, we walk the shore, until he stops, so I stop. He faces me; he snaps his fingers, and the fog clears. I recognize him. It's comforting. It's Jim Morrison; living, breathing Jim. "You're here," he says. The beach comes into focus.

Venice Beach.

I feel a presence; I look over. By my side, a white standard poodle with a blue Mohawk. The poodle licks my leg. *Wait.* I'm back in reality, in my morning, my neighborhood. As I reorient myself, I pet the dog, and its owner arrives. "Are you alright?"

My car is still on; the door is still open; the alert is still dinging. Embarrassed, I stand away from the curb. "I am, thank you." The poodle wags its tail; the man smiles. "He's a lover. His name is Valentine."

I regain composure. "What a darling name."

"It's for Henry Valentine Miller, my favorite author. Have you read him?"

"No." I'm distracted.

"Well, keep him in mind." The man collects his poodle.

"OK . . ." I respond, half-listening, half-eager to end the awkwardness.

"Take care," he good-byes.

"Same to you."

The man walks off, Valentine by his side, and I swear I hear him whistling.

La, la, la, la, la, la, la.

Outside Canter's, I park; I reassure myself, *Paris.*

Inside, I buy bagels, shmear, black-and-white cookies. At the register, I flip through a photo book. Guns N' Roses. To the images, "November Rain" plays through my mind. When I return to my car, I notice another car, a stunning Porsche 356A. As I admire the details, I'm rocked by the license plate.

VNCBCH.

40

"HELLO?"

"Grace," he finally answers.

"Maxi,"—my voice quivers—"where are you?"

Yesterday, over bagels, I told Maxime about Guns N' Roses; I asked him about Venice Beach, hoping to gain clarity, without seeming . . . crazy. Forever supportive, he kissed me all over. "We'll work this out." Today, I came home from the gym, and Maxime was gone. His suitcase gone.

That was hours ago. Hours and hours. Worried, at sunset, I started calling. Calling and calling. By the time he answers, it's nighttime.

"Hello?" I ask again, with urgency.

"I'm at the airport," he says. I can hear an attendant talking.

"The airport?"

"I'm boarding my flight."

"Your flight?"

"Yes." His voice is stone cold.

"What happened?" I start to choke up.

"I'm going to Paris," he tells me. "You're going to Venice Beach."

I fall to the floor.

"Maxi, no . . ." I start crying. "No, no, no . . ."

"*Ela*, Grace,"—he remains stoic—"I love you."

"What is happening?" I'm devastated.

"It's easier this way, trust me."

"How could you?" I'm hurt. "*How could you?*" I'm enraged.

"Shhhh." He's grounded. "Trust me."

I say nothing.

"I love you," he insists.

"But you're leaving," I counter.

"For now," he says. "It's the only way."

I ball up. Empty.

"I'm not trying to hurt you," he says.

"But you are . . ." I whimper. "*You are.*"

"Grace." He grows tender. I stop crying. I hear the love in his voice.

"Yes?"

He's silent.

I'm silent.

"Go to Venice; find your peace," he says.

He hangs up.

41

WHAT HAPPENED?

I ruminate, *What happened? What happened?*

He's gone. Ghosted. From moving in together—to gone. I'm cut off. Blocked. No way to fight it.

Maxime's gone.

Mortified, I downplay the severity to my nearest and dearest. Alone, I backslide into former habits, pretending, "It's fine; I'm fine." Publicly,

I claim the split amicable. Behind closed doors, I'm devastated.

I hide.

Off pills, no taste for booze; mainly, I sleep.

I cry; I sleep; I migrate to the sofa, where I order food and binge-watch TV. I live in sleep teddies. My phone stays in airplane mode. I don't want any news from anybody. God forbid Maxime is photographed with some new fling. My house stays dark. I lose track of time. I'm hurting; I'm numb. From bedroom to living room, living room to bedroom.

Hurting.

Numb.

Heartbroken.

One day, while wallowing, I stub my toe. There's a fierce throbbing. I yelp; I pull my foot to my hands, hopping, hopping. I lose balance. "Fuck." I release my foot; I fall.

On the floor, I'm infuriated. "FUCK YOU. FUCK THIS." Through the pain, I am seething. "FUCK, FUCK, FUCK THIS."

Tranquilo, I hear my inner voice.

My college boyfriend used to soothe me that way. *Tranquilo*, it repeats. My body relaxes. The pain subsides, and I sit up, facing the lower rungs of my bookshelf. Right then, right there, I see *Walden*, Lance's gift, never read. Without thought, I remove the book; I take it to the sofa; I start reading.

I keep reading.

Over those pages, I am restored. I shower. I dress. I open the blinds. Light. I open the windows. Air. Soon, I'm exercising. Cooking. Talking to family, friends. Reconnecting. Rehabilitating. All the while, reading.

Moving on.

By the end of the book, I'm no longer asking, *What happened?* I'm preparing. *What now?* As if Lance knew, *Walden* saved me. From Henry David Thoreau, comfort.

"Simplify, simplify."

First, I downsize, finding a minimal one-bedroom in Venice Beach. Second, I give notice on my rented Hollywood Craftsman. Third, Wallace arrives with set designers. Per her instructions, I place pink Post-its on items I want to keep. The rest . . . goes.

"Are you sure?" she asks.

"Very," I say with a hug. "Thank you."

On Wallace's command, her team dismantles my home, piece by piece, removing the remnants of my married life, off to stage a movie. It happens quickly, sealed with a check. *Sold.* More funds. More freedom.

And away the studio truck lurches.

Done.

It's my last night in my Hollywood bungalow. To honor the ending, I open the last bottle of Italian wine from my parents' birthday gift from two years ago, when I turned thirty-three. I kiss the label; I retrieve a crystal glass. Red wine in hand, I stroll through boxes, reflecting. My initial leap landed me in a net of celebrity, travel, sexiness. Glamour started the path; now, it's time for a detour.

Through less, more.

Think minimal, not martyr. I'm taking a luxury mattress and fine linens. Six Milo Baughman chairs. A glass breakfast table. A sectional sofa. My books. A flat-screen TV. Framed art and photography. Plus, family silver, crystal, china. So no, not full Thoreau, but a marked change.

Walden chic.

On my survey of simplicity, I find my trunk. Lid up. Staring down, I see twelve journals. It's the transcripts of my inner monologue, plus a first attempt at a first book, hand-written. I blow a kiss; I continue to the living room. It's June; it's gloomy, so I light the fireplace. Soon, flames dance up vintage, chevron brick. "I'll miss this," I say. Then, I fix a fireside picnic for my wine. Prosciutto, Manchego, grapes, more. I start to eat, but something's missing.

My journals.

From the trunk, I retrieve all twelve volumes, for review. Once settled, I visit Journal No. 1. At random, I flip to a page in the beginning, the middle, the end. As I do, my face scrunches at the "Woe is me." I carry on. I scan journal to journal, in hope of gold. Halfway in, I realize I'm on a misguided mission. Gold wasn't the point. These words weren't to review, but to heal. After entry, they expired. Same with the book. The story of another woman. A prior me.

I stop reading; I savor my wine, my cheese.

Music, I decide. And from a portable Marshall speaker, I shuffle rock and roll, raising volume to the Who.

"Baba O'Riley."

Opening notes accompany soft shadows on my blank walls. I stand; I remove the brass fireplace screen. I feel heat on my legs. I step back; I reach for a journal; I open it; I tear a fistful of pages from the spine.

"Good-bye," I say.

I toss the pages into the fire.

The paper burns, crumples, and I watch cobalt blue penmanship disintegrate, leaving ash. It's dramatic, but it brings me relief. Catharsis. And so, I burn it all.

Journal by journal, the flames intensify in size, shape, hue. At one point, there's a luminescent green. I've never seen a green flame. Sitting cross-legged, I admire the passing of my trauma. It gleams. Eventually, I reach the final page. I hold it close, then, I drop it in, delicately, definitively, my eyes locked as the paper disappears.

Going. Gone.

A fiery completion.

Done.

42

BIRDS CHIRP.

They're in the lemon trees.

I wake, slowly, envisioning my day. Moving day.

One last time, I run my neighborhood. Though it is early, many neighbors have started their weekend. Up the street, a puppy leads a family. Two teenagers hold hands. A retired professor gathers his newspaper. "Morning, Grace."

I smile. I wave.

At the corner, sprinklers mist a lawn. For fun, I run into the spray, which casts rainbows, making me think of a song. Across the lawn, I cue the Rolling Stones.

"She's a Rainbow."

To the tune, I sprint. At the intersection, at Melrose, I stop. I look right, left. I sprint. When the song ends, I'm by a white picket fence adorned with red roses. I stop. I inhale the fragrance. *This is it*, my mind notes. *The beauty. Follow the beauty. Trust the beauty. You're here to highlight life's beauty.*

Immediately, I tap the thoughts into my iPhone. Then, I repeat the song. I sprint. Upbeat piano and colorful lyrics push me to my finish line, a coffee shop. There, I see Moses. He treats my pour-over. "When's the move?"

"Today."

"No shit."

"I know."

"You got a spot to run to in Venice?"

"Not yet."

"Menotti's."

"Coffee?"

"And vinyl."

"Into it."

"Tell them I sent you."

"You're the best."

 A moment passes. Moses hugs me, close.

"Text before you go?" he asks.

"Will do."

I head out the swinging door; I look back; I raise my coffee. "Thank you."

K. E. GREGG

All packed, I message Moses, "It's happening."

No reply.

Minutes later, the roar of motorcycles. Moses and three friends, from his crew. At my house, Moses lifts his visor. "Brought a motorcade." Behind him, someone jokes, "Four Horsemen of the Apocalypse." Another says, "Can't believe you're leaving, Grace."

I blow them kisses. "Relax, you love the beach."

They rev. An adoring rev. To their love, I start my car; I open the sunroof; I cue Led Zeppelin. On Jimmy Page's guitar, we roll out; I follow the choppers to Sunset, then, down to the beach. At the ocean, I turn left; they turn right. I honk my horn. They rev.

We part.

Wind in my hair, I ride Pacific Coast Highway, passing wild-flower hills, coastal houses, beach clubs, approaching the roller coaster and Ferris wheel. At my exit, Bonzo thumps "Moby Dick," drumming me . . .

Home.

Part Three

43

WIND CHIMES.

An ocean breeze. Hummingbirds. Venice Beach.

Having cleared all my commitments, I start Monday morning, free. Over the week, I unpack my boxes, I settle into my Walden. On Friday, my phone rings; it's Isla. "Babe, I'm outside. I came to cook you dinner."

In L.A., no small feat. Evening traffic from Los Feliz to Venice meant an hour on the road. At least. Even so, Isla oohs and ahhs into my place, bright-eyed, bearing superfoods. "I can feel it," she says, "something special will happen here."

"I hope so," I say, opening wine, and to Buena Vista Social Club, Isla cooks a nourishing meal. Before eating, I set the table with my finest wares. China, crystal, silver. As we sit, I light long-stem candles; "Chan Chan" plays.

"How romantic," Isla notes.

"One big romance," I say. "That's the goal."

"Yes."

Hours later, we're eating strawberries, dark chocolate, when Isla asks, "Have you ever had a sound healing?"

"A what?"

"I know." She laughs. "It's different, but good different."

"Where?"

"That's the thing," she says, "up the street."

"My street?"

"Yes."

"Should I try it?"

"Seems meant to be," she says.

"Why not?" I laugh.

She sends a text.

It's set.

44

I WALK A PATH, THROUGH A GARDEN.

At the baby blue house, an open door. "Come in," a voice invites. I take off my shoes; a gong sounds; he appears. "I'm Nate." He's wearing Princeton Basketball shorts and a James Perse T-shirt. He's athletic; he resembles a young Robert Redford. "Grace." I shake his hand, and my face must have given me away, because he asks, "Not what you expected?"

"Not sure what to expect," I say.

"Tea?" he asks.

"Please."

His home is minimal, masculine, with surfboards, plants. He leads me to a sunroom, where I sit atop Guatemalan floor cushions. "Make yourself at home," he says, excusing himself to prepare the tea.

A kettle whistles. Another gong. Nate returns, holding a wooden tray with a clay-fired tea set. Afternoon filters through sheer curtains, and he pours "a custom blend for relaxation."

"Will I vomit or hallucinate?" I half-joke.

"No," he says, "not that kind of party."

He's cool. And he shares a breath exercise: "Imagine a golden ball, the size of a quarter, an inch or two below your belly button."

"OK."

"Keep your focus there, breathe in, two, three, four.

"Hold, two, three, four, five, six, seven.

"Breathe out, two, three, four, five, six, seven, eight."

A few cycles later, I'm relaxed. Sipping soundly.

"What was that?" I ask.

"A breath pattern to lower your heart rate," he says. "I use it before bed."

"How did you get into this?"

He refills my tea. He tells me about Princeton, playing basketball, double majoring in Economics, Religion. At school, he kept his faith to himself. He enjoyed an eating club, travel. After graduation, EuroLeague basketball. Barcelona. In Spain, life soared; faith seemed superfluous. Then, he tore his right Achilles. Eyes on the prize, he rehabilitated. Second game back, he tore his left Achilles. "I got the message," he says. "I ignored the message."

Basketball ended, but Nate kept his tempo. Full throttle. He deferred a Harvard MBA to join his brothers in New York. Together, they launched a private equity firm. To celebrate, they headed to Brazil, for the beaches, the women, and a quick jaunt into the Amazon. Mid-jungle, Nate happened upon a tiny enclave, where a shaman lived, in near isolation.

"Plot twist," I say.

"Wait for it . . ." He raises his tea. "My brothers returned to New York. I stayed with that shaman, for a year."

I freeze.

"It was aggressive," he acknowledges. "People thought I'd lost my mind. And I did . . . my intense monkey mind. The anxiety I carried for years, which I'd been medicating with sports, achievement, sex."

My stomach relaxes. "I see."

"I figured," he says, "otherwise, you'd have left at the first gong."

We laugh.

"So now, you're a sound healer?"

"For friends," he says. "I learned it from the shaman; it calms me, why not share it?"

"Cool."

"I try to live a balanced life. I work with my brothers, remotely, and I surf."

"A sound-healing, finance, surfing, Princeton man," I say, wrapping my mind around it.

"On paper," he says.

"On paper," I correct myself.

"We're more than our pedigrees."

After tea, I'm in a hammock, which he's stretched across the sunroom. On the floor, by my head, an arrangement of giant crystal singing bowls. He draws blackout curtains; he drapes me in a blanket. Next, he burns a stick of wood that smells like Christmas. "Palo santo. To clear the air."

Air cleared, he illuminates the room with candles. Finally, he switches off the lights. I'm cozy, and the scene he's set is beautiful. I tell him so, as he takes a seat behind me. "I'm glad," he says, placing both hands on the crown of my head. "Do you like music?"

"I love music."

"Nice. Think of this as tuning an instrument. I'm going to sing and play sounds that speak to the human body. It's meant to restore your optimal state."

"OK."

"If you feel uncomfortable, raise a hand."

"Will it be uncomfortable?"

"Shouldn't be. Should be like a concert. And a bath. That said, I know it's different; I know you're making yourself vulnerable, so I want you to feel safe. The key to this, the key to anything, is you."

"Thank you, Nate."

Silence.

The first bowl sounds. Its hum reverberates within me. He adds more bowls. Harmony. Then, he chants, in the style of monks, "*Om.*" From the tips of my toes to the crown of my head, I tingle with timelessness. I close my eyes; my lips curl. Near the end, I feel weightless, out of body.

Happy.

At the height of my sensations, the sounds dwindle. Lower. Slower. Silence. I lie in the quiet, flying, soaring. I've forgotten where I am, when he places his hands on my shoulders to ground me. "Grace."

"Yes?"

"How are you?"

"Wonderful." I stretch.

He opens the curtains; he exits the room.

Magic hour.

I'm entirely relaxed when he returns with a bowl of watermelon. The taste is unreal. I giggle, like a child. When I finish, he helps me out of the hammock, back to the floor cushions.

"Better?" he asks.

"Much," I say. "Not sure I get what you did . . ."

"Enjoyment is enough." He sits beside me. "Don't let logic trap you."

"What do you mean?"

"Overthinking," he says. "I used to intellectualize everything. I assumed that I had to understand something for it to work. That slowed my roll . . . Intuition often precedes explanation."

"Like Galileo," I say. My go-to example of awareness before proof.

"Like Galileo." He smiles. "Also, meditation, mindfulness. For ages, Eastern cultures have meditated. Now, Western science verifies the benefits."

I lower my glass. "Should I be meditating?"

"I like it."

"What about mindfulness?"

"Mindfulness is the jam," he jokes. "You're already doing it. It's the way you ate that watermelon. Entirely focused. When you're eating, really taste. When you're listening, really listen. As you do, you'll notice your thoughts. Often, they're racing, escaping the moment."

During his explanation, I'm thinking, *He knows a lot. I hope we'll be friends.* I catch myself. I laugh to Nate. "My thoughts are racing as you speak."

"Good." He smiles. "You're aware. That means you can bring your mind back to focus, gently, like training a puppy. Over time, you gain peace."

"What if there's no focus?"

"Use your breath," he says, "or numbers, words. Inhale, exhale. Peace, love. Whatever does it for you."

He crosses the room. "I like to use music." He flips through albums. "What brought you to Venice?"

I arch my back; I tell Nate the truth.

"Nice." He looks at me. "I've followed dreams, books, conversations, song lyrics . . ."

"So that's a thing?" I light up.

"If you want it to be." Nate selects a record. "We all have access to a higher power, the one that spins the earth and moves the tides. Call it what you want, it's ever-present, and if you tune to it, it guides you."

The sound of rain. Thunder. Keyboard. The Doors.

"Nate." I jump up.

"Riders on the Storm."

Barefoot, I'm dancing.

"Good choice?" he asks.

"The best. I have this Jim Morrison thing . . ."

"Maybe he's your shaman," Nate says.

"No way . . ."

"A shaman connects the spiritual and material worlds. Why not Jim Morrison?"

"That would be amazing."

"Jim Morrison, electric shaman," Nate proclaims.

"Yes!"

I twirl.

Nate raises the volume.

"Welcome to Venice, Grace."

45

AN EARLY RUN.

My mission: Menotti's, Moses's recommendation. Coffee.

Along the way, a change in plans, my inner voice: *Go to the Canals.*

And so, I head inland, to developer Abbot Kinney's ode to Venice, Italy. When I enter the oasis, I silence my music; I take in morning. Beside me, still waters resemble Impressionist paintings. I stare into reflections of palm trees, rowboats, canoes. Crossing a footbridge, I hear, "Grace!"

Authoritative, yet sweet.

"Grace!"

At close distance, I recognize, "Wes!" My Navy SEAL, from Manhattan Beach, from hurricane relief. I sprint to him; he's fresh off a workout, sweaty, wearing a weighted vest, in a grassy yard. He unstraps his vest; he hugs me off my feet. "Amazing Grace!"

Beside him, in his Texas drawl, Trey: "How sweet the sound!"

"You two are ridiculous," I say. "Who lives here?"

"I do." Wes beams. "Closed last month. Trey's in town for meetings."

"Fun!"

"What about you?" Trey asks.

"I live up the beach!"

"Well, neighbor,"—Wes grins—"coffee?"

"Please."

From grass to hardwood floors, I kick off my running shoes and socks. Throughout the home, roses. Dozens of roses. At my enchantment, Wes says, "Whenever I return from a mission, I fill my house with flowers. It resets me."

In the kitchen, Trey shakes a can of Copenhagen. "I'm a bubble bath man myself." Packing a lip, he tells me, "Lavender bubbles, Himalayan sea salt."

"Yes," Wes concurs. "Grace, you been there?"

I shake my head. "I can't remember my last bubble bath. I can't remember my last roses."

Wes shakes his head. "You aren't living."

We laugh; Wes grinds coffee beans. While I wait, I allow my mind to wander—2012, Rockaway Beach. *Never alone*, my thoughts warm me, when Trey brings me back—"Earth to Grace."

I look up.

"Your coffee." He hands me a mug.

"Thank you." I smell the aroma. "I was thinking about when we met."

Trey softens. "Instant family."

"For life," Wes adds, turning on the TV. "Want to watch swimming?"

"The Olympics?" I ask.

"Yes ma'am."

"Please."

There, on the screen, a name flashes below a starting block.

"Is that . . . ?" I confirm.

"Sure is," Trey says.

It's our buddy, who volunteered with us after Hurricane Sandy. He's on the starting block. I'm giddy. The race begins. I'm ecstatic. He finishes first. "Gold!" I shout. Next thing I know, I'm jumping on Wes's sofa. After the anthem plays, I collect my thoughts. "Two weeks together," I say, "he never mentioned a thing."

"Not his style," Trey says.

"Show, don't tell," Wes agrees.

Hero.

46

FIVE A.M.

Shutters on the Beach.

In the hotel lobby, SEALs, Rangers, Marines, some active, some veteran, all gathered together for Physical Training (PT).

"I'm nervous," I whisper to Wes, to Trey.

"You'll be fine," Wes pats my back. "We got you."

The General arrives. We follow him to the sand. Waves crash; we stretch. In my eye line, the Technicolor Ferris wheel spins against a pre-dawn sky.

Once warm, we run.

Fast.

Able, yet amateur, I drift to the back. There, I focus on Wes. For a while, his energy lifts me. Even so, I'm drifting. Apart.

Alone. For a second.

"You got this." Trey joins me, at my pace, boosting morale.

Up the beach, others take turns, rotating in and out beside me, bolstering my spirit, showing solidarity. I'm not made to feel less. I'm encouraged to be more. And it works. As this happens, I recognize that true power empowers.

At the Venice Pier, on the sun's first shine, we drop to push-ups. Ongoing reps, a game of knockout, to the last man pushing. Trey. Applause. Arms burning, I move to my core. Three sets of 100. Noticing my efforts, the General praises, "Well done, ballerina." Earlier, running by my side, he had asked my story, and clearly, he took note.

After abs, we stand for squats, lunges, jumping jacks. More running. Destination: Muscle Beach. Pull-ups, dips. I push my limits. I cheer the others on. I'm sweaty, shaky, and invigorated as we jog back to Shutters.

PT complete.

"Thank you for including me." I shake the General's hand.

"You did great," he says.

"Wish I'd been better." I kick the sand.

"Nonsense," he insists. "Never talk down to yourself or about yourself. By my watch, you stuck with it and you finished."

My spine straightens.

"That's what matters to me," he says.

"*Thank you.*" I gain confidence.

"You could have panicked, but you didn't," he says.

"You're right."

"I pay attention." He nods. Then, he leaves me with wisdom.

"Keep at it, Grace. Calm is contagious."

Already sore, I fall into my seat.

"Pancakes," I tell Wes my wish.

Soon, we're toasting orange juice over blueberry pancakes.

"That kicked my ass," I tell him, "but I'm happy about it."

"Good." Wes laughs.

Drowning his plate in syrup, Trey asks, "What do you mean by *happy*?"

That stumps me. I assumed the meaning to be self-evident. An American value, since 1776. Apparently, I hadn't done my homework. I take a buttery bite. Wes chimes in, "I like eudemonia."

"Greek?" I recognize the sound.

"Yes, for flourishing."

"Eudemonia," I test the word. I take another buttery bite.

"It's the notion that lasting happiness stems from good thoughts, good words, good deeds."

"What do you mean by *good*?" I ask.

Wes pauses; he leans back, "If it nourishes me. If it nourishes others."

"Solid," Trey agrees, to which Wes clarifies, "The *highest* me."

"Who's *he*?" I ask.

Wes rests his utensils, center plate, inverted V, "Well, there's lower me: animal, reactive, impulsive. And higher me: conscious, connected, purposeful."

"Enlightened," I say.

"In progress." He's hyper-present. "Higher me requires higher standards. Better habits. More discipline. It's an investment, but the returns are well worth it. There's this deeper pleasure."

"*Deeper pleasure*," I echo. The notion penetrates me.

Trey places a fist on the table. "Amen, brother. Hedonism's so hot right now, but I find it boring. Same old, same old. I like to push myself. Whenever I self-actualize, it's unreal."

"The buy-in isn't always easy," Wes admits, "like that four-thirty a.m. alarm."

"For sure," Trey says. "It's not comfortable, but it's powerful ... so much to gain." He turns to me. "Once I got hooked, my tolerance for discomfort soared."

"Interesting." I finish my breakfast; I place my utensils at four o'clock. Shortly thereafter, the busser clears, and I smile at him. "Thank you."

Conversation continues.

"The key is reminding myself what's on the other side," Trey says.

"It's like a hangover before the high . . ." I suggest.

"The *highest* high." Trey says.

"For your highest self." Wes grabs the check.

"Thanks, brother," Trey says. "Have y'all read Ben Franklin's *Autobiography*?"

"I have," Wes says. "Grace?"

"No."

"Not yet," Trey counters. "If you're looking to step up your routine, it's a classic."

"Cool," I say. "Thanks, guys."

Trey asks for my address, and a few clicks later, he's gifted me the book. Another resource on my path. Another guidepost.

Eudemonia.

47

"I'M COMING TO CALIFORNIA."

He tells me, over the phone. I never expected to see him again, but somewhere, I must have hoped.

Lance.

"When?"

"Next week, with the team. I have a night off; it's yours."

Now, he's on his way, and I wonder about his mood. All the way from Rio, no medal. There's a knock at the door. I greet him. He's smiling, vibing, as handsome as ever. I leap into his arms; he smells straight from the shower. I run my fingers through his damp blond hair. I cover him in kisses.

"Still like me, hey?" He laughs.

"A bit."

"I'll take it." He returns my affection.

At brunch, we sit at the counter, sharing brioche French toast, coffee—and like magnets, we snap back together. Next, the beach. Hand in hand, we dive through waves, swimming out of my depth, where Lance holds me around his waist, pointing to the horizon. "Sydney's that way."

"A quick swim," I joke.

"Whenever you miss me."

After the ocean, we sun ourselves dry, sharing stories, thoughts, life. Though much had changed, much remained the same. It's as if we evolved, together. My sexy study buddy. And true to form, he inquires, "Did you read *Walden*?"

I roll onto him. "I can't believe I didn't tell you."

"What?"

"It inspired this."

"Venice?"

"My Walden by the sea."

"Oh yeah?"

"Yes. Thoreau inspired me to simplicity. I sleep well, eat well, meditate. I run; I read; I reflect. And I journal. I document life's beauty."

"Like an athlete."

"You're right!"

"You're healthy, mindful, focused."

"It's a privilege," I say, when a twinge of guilt hits me. Rather than resist or fight, I sit with it. Soon, the guilt dissolves into purpose. "I have the luxury of contemplating life's big picture, so I am. Hopefully, I'll be able to contribute something . . . to help others."

"You do love people," he says.

"I do." I lay my head on his warm chest. *Ba-dum. Ba-dum.* For a while, he massages my back. Suddenly, I feel his chest expand, and he tells me, "You've more than read *Walden,* you're living it."

K. E. GREGG

Back home, sex, shower, shower sex, and I dress in his T-shirt. We move to the kitchen for a drink, and Lance notices the list on my fridge:

"TEMPERANCE.

Eat not to Dullness;

drink not to Elevation.

SILENCE.

Speak not but what may benefit others or yourself. Avoid trifling Conversation.

ORDER.

Let all your Things have their Places. Let each Part of your Business have its Time.

RESOLUTION.

Resolve to perform what you ought. Perform without fail what you resolve.

FRUGALITY.

Make no Expense but to do good to others or yourself: i.e. Waste nothing.

INDUSTRY.

Lose no Time. Be always employ'd in something useful. Cut off all unnecessary Actions.

SINCERITY.

Use no hurtful Deceit.

Think innocently and justly; and, if you speak, speak accordingly.

JUSTICE.

Wrong none, by doing Injuries or omitting the Benefits that are your Duty.

MODERATION.

Avoid Extremes. Forbear resenting Injuries so much as you think they deserve.

CLEANLINESS.

Tolerate no Uncleanness in Body, Cloaths, or Habitation.

TRANQUILITY.

Be not disturbed by Trifles, or at Accidents common or unavoidable.

CHASTITY.

[Enjoy] Venery; Never to Dullness, Weakness, or the Injury of your own or another's Peace or Reputation.

HUMILITY.

Imitate Jesus or Socrates."

I stand behind him, hugging him. "Benjamin Franklin's virtues."

"Old school."

"Throw-back," I joke. "I'm not all about him, but he does offer a solid foundation."

"Seems so." Lance finishes reading.

"It adds structure to my Walden."

"I like it." He turns around. "Why bracket the word enjoy?"

"I updated chastity."

"Strong edit." He pulls me into his arms. "Now what?"

"Wine?"

He lowers me; I select a bottle of chilled rosé.

"Allow me." He uncorks the wine, while I retrieve two crystal glasses.

"Walden by the beach, hey?" he asks.

"Moderation," I quote Franklin. "I'm avoiding extremes."

We flirt on the sofa, diving into philosophy. When I refill our wine, Lance surveys a stack of books, "Ralph Waldo Emerson, Marcus Aurelius, Thich Nhat Hanh, Gandhi . . ."

"They keep me company," I say.

"Heavy hitters."

"You planted the seed." I retrieve *Walden* from the bedroom. Back on the sofa, I straddle him, and I read the passage he marked for me.

With a slight edit.

"I went to [Venice Beach] because I wished to live deliberately, to front only the essential facts of life, and see if I could not learn what it had to teach, and not, when I came to die, discover that I had not lived. I did not wish to live what was not life, living is so dear; nor did I wish to practice resignation, unless it was quite necessary. I wanted to live deep and suck out all the marrow of life . . ."

"Precisely." He lifts me off the sofa. He carries me to my balcony where he lowers me. Outside, the skies are pink. Immersed in sunset, I decide, "I want to balance sucking out the marrow with telling the stories."

"Go for it."

"You." I kiss him.

"And you,"—he smiles—"do you think it's easy for men to discuss these things?"

 "I don't know."

"Not for me, not usually."

"Oh."

"*You* make it easy. You're so warm, inviting. I share things with you . . . that I don't share . . . with anybody."

I kiss him again.

He's reflecting my power back to me. Through relationship, discovery.

"Lance," I say his name with newfound appreciation.

"Yes?"

"I think I'm starting to see myself . . . the way you see me."

Next, I'm lifted onto his hips; I wrap him in my arms and legs.

He takes a breath.

And magnificently, he kisses me.

48

WAY UP HIGH.

On a park bench, we eat burritos. It's early afternoon, and from a grassy hill, we watch the beach. Soon, Lance's team will take him to the airport. Back to Australia. Oz. I finish my lunch; Lance takes my foil; he drops our trash in the bin. When he returns, he gathers his thoughts, and he faces me. "Grace," he says, "I've always dreamed of a woman whose outer beauty reveals her inner beauty. The more at peace she feels with herself, with the world, the more beautiful she becomes." I tingle. "Grace," he repeats my name, "that's you."

"Thank you. What a compliment."

"It's true."

I move onto his lap. "I want to tell you something . . ." I bite my lip; I hesitate.

"Go on," he encourages me.

"I don't know."

"Go on . . ."

My heart races; I look into his green eyes. "I love you." Not a moment passes. Entirely calm, he takes my face in his hands. "I know. I love you too."

His team arrives.

Down the hill, he walks. When he reaches the team bus, he turns.

"Good-bye!" I shout.

He shakes his head. He smiles. He waves.

"See you soon."

49

END OF SUMMER.

Lazing on my sofa, I think through simplicity. So far, my Walden has served me well. For that reason, I go deeper. No more news. No more social media.

A firm focus.

Given the year, 2016, my decision bucked the norm of Insta-snapping-tweets. *Who cares?* I know what I need. A season of silence. On that mission, I unlock my iPhone; I delete applications. No announcement. No grandstanding. A gift from me to me. A way to accelerate my listening, my learning, my growth. And with intention, I clear my screen.

"Alright." I stretch. I place my phone aside.

Off the grid, I prepare to level up. In jean shorts, tank, no bra, I spend the evening reading *Return to Tipasa*, the English translation, Camus. There, I find an articulation of my desire, what I hope to gain from my Walden.

"No matter how hard the world pushes against me, within me, there's something stronger—something better, pushing right back.

"An invincible summer."

50

HUMAN TOUCH.

Twenty-one days unplugged, and I crave human connection. Specifically, human touch. To be fair, Thoreau hails from another time. As for me, I'm a hugger.

Concerned, I call Isla. "Have I gone too far?"

"No." She laughs. "Take a break."

Days later, I'm at the Roxy. A concert.

Inside the theater, I enter the heat of a crowd; I look for Isla. Along my search, a man bumps into me. "Pardon." He stops. We stare at each other. Then, without introduction or reservation, we hug.

A deep hug. A long hug. Nearly twenty seconds.

Afterward, he extends his hand, and I notice a British accent. "Easton Wylde."

"Grace."

He raises his hat. His dimples appear on the tips of a wide smile. We don't say much, if anything, and again, we hug.

"Lovely to meet you," he says. I spot Isla; I place a hand on Easton's heart before walking off. "Take care." When I reach Isla, she throws her arms around me. "How do you know *Easton Wylde*?"

"I don't." I laugh. "Why are you saying his name that way?"

"Babe, he's on fire."

"I've been offline . . ."

"His new album is *so* you," she says, and delighted, she recounts what she observed, "You don't know him, and yet, I find you hugging him."

"It felt right . . ."

"You're such a lover." She smiles. "He must be too."

"I'm here for the human touch," I joke, and inside, I'm grateful.

"Well then,"—she wraps her arm around me—"let's go."

After the show, above the Roxy, a party.

Isla entertains clients; I step away. On the outskirts of the crowd, I pull out the bench of a tiny white piano. I sit. I cross my legs. I hear my name: "Grace."

"Easton."

"May I?"

"Please."

He sits. Comfortably. Close. And he asks, "What are you drinking?"

"Soda water, made to look like a cocktail."

"Sober?" he asks.

"No, but on a mission." I tap my chest. "That inner journey."

"That explains it . . ."

"What?"

"You have a beautiful aura."

I've lived in Venice long enough to know what he means, my energy. And he's genuine; it's not a line; it's not put on; he's making himself vulnerable. There's intimacy. In response, I lean in. "You see me."

"I do."

He's cool, and he taps the bench. "They say John Lennon played this piano."

"Peace," I say, under my breath, as he lifts the piano lid. We swivel around, and my fingers caress the keys. Beside me, Easton starts a melody. To his tune, I stare out sweaty windows, admiring a whirl of lights on the Sunset Strip. When Easton finishes his melody, we swivel back.

His leg touches mine.

Next, he removes his hat, placing it on his lap, and I notice a matchstick tucked in the band. Armor off, he shakes his long hair. In the process, light catches his necklace, a cross. He takes the cross in his hand, and gently, he twists it, beneath his undone shirt. Looking over, I read a tattoo on his wrist: BE KIND.

There it is. Our link. By now, my energy is in his energy; I'm amplified. As if feeling the same thing, he drapes his arm around me.

"Have we met before?" he asks.

"Not in this life," I flirt.

"Maybe on the other side."

"Maybe. May I ask you something? Something real?"

"Please."

"What do you value?"

Immediately, he answers, "Freedom."

"Me too." I rest my head on his shoulder. "And love."

"The one enhances the other, don't you think?"

"I do."

Before we can continue, a team of handlers approaches. "Easton! Where have you been?"

"Apologies," he says. "Needed a sec."

"Quick photo by the bar," they say.

"Be right over."

The handlers vanish; Easton replaces his hat; Easton stands. "See you soon, love."

He leaves.

For a while, I watch him do his thing. Then, I'm ready to return to the beach. I hug Isla good night; I leave.

Outside, Sunset is a blur, pulsing with people, places, parties. I call a car; the driver directs me up a side street. As I make my way, I hear a voice. "Love."

"Easton."

"Grace."

"Going?"

"Yes, a car is on its way."

"Keep you company?"

"Please."

He escorts me away from the scene. Above us, a full moon and flowering trees. Jacaranda. Again, Easton drapes his arm around me. He feels like the boy next door, which prompts my question, "How do you handle the fame?"

"Ahhh, yes," he says. "It's interesting."

"I bet."

"Well . . ." he starts, "it's not about me, is it? It's about connection. We all want to be part of something, something bigger than ourselves. For whatever reason, I give people that. It's an honor."

"Hadn't thought of it that way."

"Don't get me wrong, it can be a lot. I have to be careful, so it doesn't consume me. Last year, I went to Thailand, stayed with monks, nobody knew me for miles. That did wonders for the soul. When you strip away the nonsense, we're all the same. Aren't we?"

"We are."

My energy spikes.

My car approaches.

With care, Easton tucks me in the back seat, but before going, he pulls a notebook from his pocket. Unhurriedly, he writes; he tears out the page; he bends down; he takes purple petals from the sidewalk. Finally, he folds the page in two, pressing the jacaranda flower, and placing his note in my hand. "Call me. You can call me tomorrow. You can call me next week. You can call me next year . . . but please, call."

I'm about to answer, but he closes the door; he taps the car.

I go.

Simmering, I rub my thumbs across textured paper, and I ask the driver for a scenic route: from West Hollywood to the coast, then, onto Venice. Down Sunset, I wait. Past the Beverly Hills Hotel, past UCLA, through Brentwood, through the Palisades, I wait. When I reach the ocean, I open my note. Beneath the flower, he's written his number and an Italian phrase.

Se son rose fioriranno.

If they are roses, they will bloom.

51

FRESH-GROOMED SAND.

Up the beach, I sprint. At the Venice Breakwater, I watch surfers dance longboards to shore. All the while, Easton's on my mind. He's magic, but this season is for me. And so, I breathe him in, out, over the ocean.

Release.

After PT, I cross the boardwalk to a murmuration. Foggy skies. Up the alley, on a mural, Jim Morrison towers shirtless, painted in his leathers against an orange façade. My electric shaman, my rock angel, keeping watch, immortalized by art.

Near Jim, Menotti's. Through the swinging door, I remove my sunglasses and AirPods. Once present, my eyes land on a bistro table, on a man. I blink at the likeness. Jim Morrison reincarnate. A young Jim. An innocent Jim.

Sweet, contemplative, alone.

Lost in thought, he gazes through me, slowly tapping his foot, as if keeping time. He chews the end of a ballpoint pen, until his foot stops; he begins to write. Line after line spills from his hand, as his lips follow along, tracing introspection.

I collect my dark roast, and instead of going, I sit. At a table. By his side. Unaware of my company, he writes, ardently, one long thought, until he drops his pen. He finishes his coffee.

He places the mug aside.

My eyes turn to his belongings. Near his journal, a stack of weathered books, Aldous Huxley, James Baldwin, Jack Kerouac. The trappings of an old soul. Respectfully, I turn away, but a rustling brings me back. With purpose, he searches, pulling a crumpled, typewritten page from his bag. Relieved, he reads the page. Once, twice, satisfied.

At that, I unlock my iPhone; I start writing a story. It's a remarkable response, the first of its kind. In a stream, my thumbs tap letters onto the screen, stringing words together, honestly, in tender tribute. The flow continues, creating a portrait that pours from another place. Effortlessly. And as suddenly as it starts, it stops.

Transmission complete.

I take a breath. My chest raises, charged, fulfilled. At the top of my breath, I see that *he* is watching me. Our eyes connect. He nods. I'm touched. Afterward, he packs his belongings; he heads for the door. In the frame, he looks back; he flashes me a sign.

Peace.

Out of Menotti's, into the daylight, I walk.

At Windward Circle, a dozen heart-shaped balloons twist in the breeze, tied to a lamppost. Rather than continue my usual route, I veer off at the balloons. A post office. A church. A picket fence with climbing roses. By my mood, I follow a side street shaded by palm trees. On the asphalt, in large block letters, the street has been painted:

I

LOVE

YOU.

My Love Street, I smile to myself. I look to the sky. "Thank you." Without a car in sight, I walk across the letters in the style of Thich Nhat Hanh—my feet kissing the earth. Finally, I cue the Doors, every cell in my body swirling.

La, la, la, la, la, la, la.

52

ELECTION DAY.

I vote.

Discreetly. Privately. According to my values.

Back home, I make another election. Self-love. To maintain my calm. To ground my kindness. To pass it on. No matter what the ballots decide, I will live my truth.

And from that place, I write; I write; I write.

53

ALMOST THANKSGIVING.

It's Monday, and I cruise up PCH.

First stop: Malibu. A breakfast burrito. Among surfers, I enjoy cheesy, avocado goodness, bundled in November sun. One surfer tells me, "Rincon's firing." According to his directions, I detour; I watch the waves for a while. Next stop: Santa Barbara. I order a flat white from a local roaster by the Mission. The coffee shop is filled with cyclists, clicking and clacking in cleats. Taking my drink to go, I stroll the Mission yard. Then, I carry on.

Sunroof open, music blasting, Highway 1.

Slowly, a gloom descends. On its chill, I turn up my seat warmer; I wrap a scarf around my neck. Between cities, before the rush, I'm making great time. Not a care in the world, when all of a sudden, a force comes knocking. A feeling. One I don't like. And it hits me like a Mack truck.

Flustered, I reach for peppermint gum. A sip of water. I focus on my breath. To no avail. The feeling is fierce. It conquers the pit of my stomach. It fills my chest, tensing my neck, clenching my jaw, ready to erupt.

Anger.

White-knuckling the wheel, I pull over at a scenic viewpoint. Fortunately, I'm alone. With the landing to myself, a song comes to mind, one I hadn't heard since college— "Killing in the Name," Rage Against the Machine. Once I cue the track, I throw off my seat belt; I raise the volume. It's me, the music, the cliffs, the ocean. It's me, the music, the cliffs, the ocean, and *anger*. Hot, hot anger, ripping through me, to song. At first, I'm nodding to the lyrics, but as the song builds, my fury builds. Soon, I'm shaking my hair, convulsing, and on the outro, I explode. I SCREAM.

At the top of my lungs.

"FUCK YOU!"

Slamming the wheel.

"FUCK YOU!!!"

I'm unleashed.

The music grants me cover, to be upset. No provocation, only angry because I needed to be angry. It's long overdue, and its suppression is harming me. No more. There, on that scenic overlook, I invite years of pent-up poison to rise up. To be freed.

Motherfucker.

The song ends; I run it back. I pull my hair into a samurai knot. I rage again.

Yes.

Then, it passes. I turn off the music; I gain understanding. If faced responsibly, anger's no enemy, no destroyer, but a feeling, as valid as any other. Part of life, the totality. When anger rises up, I need not act, but welcome it, informing my mind, unburdening my soul, creating space . . . for relief.

Recomposed, I return to the road. As I drive, I break through the gloom, reaching a spot of sunshine. On my right, an emerald green sign.

HARMONY

Pop. 18

Charmed, I take the exit. It leads me to an enclave of artists. I get out; I make the rounds. Hand-blown glass. Pottery. Up the hill, a winemaker. Outside the tasting room, I overlook the valley. It's breathtaking, plus, it's affirming. After anger . . .

Harmony.

54

ABOVE THE CLOUDS.

I reach the bluffs of Big Sur. Towering grasses, gliding hawks, Rothko skies painted into the Pacific. I follow a trail of sunshine along tree-covered cliffs. Redwoods. Through the sunroof, I inhale pristine air, and around a bend, I notice a wooden arch.

HENRY MILLER MEMORIAL

On impulse I park. No other cars, but a dove blue Volkswagen bus. Beside the VW, a sign:

HENRY MILLER

MEMORIAL LIBRARY

BOOKS MUSIC ART

OPEN

My steps crunch on sequoia needles. *Why do I know this name?*

The poodle.

The Mohawk.

The author.

Yes. Through the arch, confirmation on a plaque: Henry Valentine Miller. Here, a memorial to a man who didn't believe in memorials.

I'm baited.

Curious, I pass through the redwoods, noticing an outdoor piano, camping tents, clothes drying on a line. To my right, a grassy field, strung with lights, headlined by a movie screen. Up ahead, an understated cabin, where cats sunbathe and campers converse over coffee. The cabin is open, so I enter. It's a library, a bookshop, filled with Miller memorabilia—photos, letters, typewriters, essays, novels.

Of all my reading, I rarely touch novels. My tastes lean toward nonfiction, real life, real stories. Until . . . Henry Miller. Quickly, I see that he wrote in both worlds, that he blended both worlds. Miller embraced the novel for its freedom. In that format, he merged experience with understanding, employing fiction to convey life's essence, to communicate truths, perspective, philosophy. And he wasn't alone. A section of his memorial is devoted to similar novelists doing similar things.

Fascinating.

From title to title, I learn he's a man of controversy, his work once banned in the United States, too racy. In many ways, he propelled progress; unfortunately, beneath his ideals, spots of sexist, racist, offensive language, a sign of his time, I suppose. Not right, not at all, but part of a whole. A man, on the way to himself. And so, rather than cancel him, I look for growth. I seek the beauty beyond his flaws, as I would want done for me. After all, none of us is perfect. Evolution is the goal.

Craving more, I select a number of Miller's books for purchase. First, *The Colossus of Maroussi*, which takes me to Greece, then, *Quiet Days in Clichy*, which takes me to France. From there, I'm drawn to his memoir, *Big Sur and the Oranges of Hieronymus Bosch*. Finally, I choose a compilation, *Henry Miller on Writing*. At the vintage register, a clerk asks, "Are you a writer?"

"I write . . ." I answer, thinking of New York, my journals, my notes.

"Do you enjoy it?"

"Yes."

"Well then, you're a writer."

My chest rises; I feel oddly ordained, as he completes the transaction. In parting, he suggests another stop, "Big Sur Bakery."

Up the road, I find the bakery. In its lot, the dove blue VW. This time, its owners are lounging by the bus.

"Beautiful Volkswagen," I say. "I saw it at the Henry Miller library."

"How I love Henry Miller," the woman greets me.

"I haven't read him yet," I tell her.

"You're in for a treat," the man says. "Are you a writer?"

"I am."

"What do you write?" he asks.

"Stories," I answer, simply.

"Nothing better." The woman claps. "Live big; write the stories; share them far and wide."

"OK." My heart likes the sound of that mission.

"Taste it all," the man says.

"*Savor* it all," the woman clarifies.

"I will," I promise.

They treat me to cinnamon scones.

With art, wine, books, and baked goods, I travel from Big Sur, through Carmel, Monterey, onward, accompanied by sunset. Then, darkness. A pure abyss, which consumes a stretch before introducing San Francisco's city lights. When I reach Lombard Street, I turn up a steep hill to my brother's condo in Pacific Heights. Dressed in business casual, he helps me navigate the sharp descent to his guest parking space. Out of the car, I stretch, and I hug him. "Loyal!"

He grabs my weekender, hoisting the bag over his shoulder, "What's in this, books?"

He's joking, but he's spot on.

Books.

55

THANKSGIVING.

In Napa, we're talking spatchcock. Turkey.

It's me, Loyal, and Loyal's girlfriend, Dechen, hosted by my childhood friend Page and her husband, Matt. Not ready to face the East Coast, I confided in Loyal, who planned a California Friendsgiving.

Over pâté, I describe my life in Venice. "It's simple, really. Mindfulness. Meditation. Walks. Journaling." As I talk, I hear dramatic differences from my political, partying, and jet-setting days. Fortunately, Dechen relates. "Sounds like Kathmandu." Dechen grew up in Nepal; her family is Tibetan Buddhist, and a lama, a teacher of dharma, named her. In Tibetan, Dechen means "great bliss."

I want to hear more.

Dechen tells me about her walking meditations with her grandmother in Kathmandu. Together, they walk around the Boudha Stupa, a Buddhist shrine and gathering place. Their ritual speaks to my ritual, so I ask Dechen for a mantra, a way to enhance my walks.

"What kind?" she asks.

I pause. It comes to me. "Something to send calm to everyone, from transient teens to stressed tech founders."

She pauses. It comes to her, "*Om mani padme hum.*"

The sound soothes me, and although that's enough, I ask what it means.

"It's a mantra for transformation," she says. "It heals and calms. It fosters compassion for all beings. Through repetition, it purifies the mind; it strengthens inner wisdom, inner peace."

"Beautiful." I smile. Will you help me pronounce it?"

"Of course." She slows her words, "Ohm . . . mah-nee . . . pahd-may . . . hoom."

And together, we practice.

All of us.

Later, in the kitchen, I help Page with the meal.

"How did you do it?" I ask her.

"The potatoes?"

"The move from consulting to chef."

"Oh." She washes her hands.

A couple years ago, Page used a sabbatical from her company to attend culinary school in Napa. There, she fell in love with a winemaker. She became a chef. She never went back.

"Life's short." She grabs a dish towel. "I bet on myself."

"It worked out." I top stuffing with fresh herbs.

"You forget the transition period." She laughs. "Not everybody got it. Not everybody gets it. So what?"

"So what," I agree.

"It's the only way."

"I needed to hear that; my ego's been struggling."

To Page, I admit the strain behind my serenity—much of my self-esteem had been tied to jobs, relationships, possessions, status. When stripped bare, I struggled. My soul soared, but my confidence struggled. What's more, in certain circles, my decisions diminished my worth.

"Never," Page intercedes. "*You* decide your worth."

"You're right."

"Never forget that. *You* know what's best for you. If people disagree, that's their business. And frankly, none of your business."

"Wow," I say.

"Too tough?" she asks.

"Just right." I hug her.

"We've got so much to be thankful for," she reminds me. "I mean . . . look at that spatchcock." She laughs. Our turkey's brined, flattened, golden brown.

"Shall we carve it?" I ask.

"Yes. Matt's in the wine cellar . . . would Loyal?"

"Absolutely." Loyal responds, as he enters the kitchen with Dechen.

"Everything's working out," I say.

"Always does." Page hands Loyal an apron.

The carving begins. Soon, Matt returns. Sparkling red wine pops. Lambrusco. Matt fills our glasses; Page proposes a toast, "*Om mani padme hum.*"

Dinner is served.

56

FRIDAY NIGHT.

A post-Thanksgiving party. For Movember, in support of men's health.

Our group costume: *Magnum, P.I.* At the entry, we pose for a photo, forming a rainbow of Hawaiian shirts, paired with aviators and fake Tom Selleck 'staches.

Matt's winery hosts the party. On the dance floor, hit follows hip-hop hit, until the DJ takes a breather. During the break, we step back to people-watch. A group of friends enters; I do a double take.

"Who is that?" I ask Page. "In the captain's hat?"

"That is a unicorn," she says. "I've never seen him or anyone like him in town."

To our laughter, Loyal asks, "What's the good word?" Smitten, I gesture at the unicorn.

"Tall dark rocker guy?" he asks.

"Yes."

"Go say hey."

"No." I blush, and the DJ spins Blackstreet, Dr. Dre, Queen Pen. Relieved, I grab Page's hand, and we return to dance floor safety.

"No Diggity." No doubts.

A few songs later, I want a drink. Waiting on service, I re-knot my floral shirt.

"Hot out there?" a man asks.

"Just me," I zing, whipping around to . . . tall dark rocker guy. "Oh." I flush; I recover. "Hello, Captain."

"Actually, I'm Yacht Rock." He tips his hat.

"Yacht Rock!" I touch his arm, riding a wave of nostalgia.

We banter a bit, and bartender's intuition delivers two shots. Tequila. I lick the top of my thumb; the Captain dashes it with salt. Lick—shot—lime. Tingling with agave, I ask, "What are you into?"

"Music. In real life, I'm a musician."

"Fun! What type of music?"

"Rock. I'm in a band."

"Rock! What are you called?"

"Not sure you've heard of us . . ."

"Try me."

SLAM.

At his answer, I slam the bar. Both hands.

"NO."

"Yes."

I'm stunned. I think of Jack, of my Echo Park days. With emotion, I confess, "Your music got me through a tough time. In particular, that first song, on your first album."

"I'm honored." He smiles.

As he looks at me, I feel vulnerable, exposed. In response, I backslide to distrust. "Wait. Are you fucking with me?"

"About my band? That'd be weird." He's confused.

"Did that guy put you up to this?" I point to Loyal, who is high-stepping and funky-piano-dancing with Dechen.

The Captain shakes his head. "No, but I like his style."

My mind churns; I rip off my mustache. "Prove it."

Next, I take his hand; I march him away from the party, into the vines. He's far taller than me, but he doesn't pull back; he's curious, lighthearted. You'd think his mood would quell my concerns. It doesn't. Still doubting, I grab my iPhone. "Alright, Mister."

"Alright." He adjusts his hat.

I locate the song. I press play. The intro unfolds . . . he sings. My mouth widens. Mortified. *It's him. My God, it's him.* Staring into my eyes, he sings, holding my attention, shifting my mood from alarm to gratitude. *It's him. My God, it's him.*

Softening his gaze, he finishes his song. The entire song.

I stop the music; I throw my arms around him. "You have no idea how much this means to me." After our hug, I bring my hands to his arms, and he lowers his head. "I think I might. You're shaking."

"I am . . ." I start to apologize, but he intervenes.

"Sometimes we doubt. It happens. How cool that I got to dismantle your doubt. I hope you keep this in mind."

"I will."

The Captain looks at my iPhone. "I'm guessing you know the words?"

"I do."

"Want to sing with me?"

"I do!"

And so, it happens, impossible to predict, impossible to deny, a playful encore, under a slice of moon, in Napa vines. As I sing, I recall the Rock God, the wisdom from Chateau, *No coincidences.*

Life is looking out for me.

K. E. GREGG

57

FOGHORNS BLARE.

Monday morning, tucked in bed, I wake to a view of the Bay. Sleepy, back in San Francisco, I cozy under down. Up the hallway, I smell coffee brewing; bacon sizzling; eggs scrambling, low and slow.

Dechen and Loyal start their workweek.

On my own schedule, I meditate, then I dress to run. Well-timed, I leave the condo with my brother, hugging him good-bye. "I love you. See you at Christmas."

I walk downhill. At the light, I sprint through Cow Hollow, through the Marina, passing Edwardian homes decked for the holidays. At the water, I admire docked boats en route to Crissy Field. On a dirt path splitting beach from grass, I approach the fog-dressed bridge, reaching my finish line—Fort Point. There, I watch surfers ride the break, slowly, steadily, in a frame of International Orange steel. Next, PT, and return sprints, past cypress trees, where neighbors play fetch with dogs. Goldens. Aussies. Rescues.

Spirits high, I sweat out the weekend, slowing to a walk, on Chestnut Street. At a corner, I spot the "Nuthouse," where Page lived with friends, in our twenties. At its steps, I relive theme parties, beer pong, flip cup, Jell-O shots, and the night we drove to Vegas. Why? Because I'd never been. Hopped up on highlights, I enter a coffee shop; it's bustling with khaki and fleece, young professionals ready to tech over the world. The line moves quickly, and soon, I sip an almond milk cappuccino, sprinkled with cinnamon.

I climb the hill; I take a hot shower; I hit the road.

It's after rush hour, so I fly south to French art-pop. By Half Moon Bay, I crave a beverage. Something hot, festive. On instinct, I find a local spot, where surfers brew drinks, forecasting swell. When I receive my hot chocolate, I ask, "Where can I watch the waves?"

"Mavericks," the first's voice elongates his answer.

"It's not that big today," the second notes.

"Where are you from?" the first asks.

"Venice Beach."

"Ever seen a big break?"

"No."

"Go to Mavericks," they conclude in unison.

A short drive later, I walk to the edge. *My God.*

"Not that big" blows my mind. I plant my feet; I drink my hot chocolate. To start, the water rolls in blue, dreamy. Then, momentum builds, a wave takes shape. Taller. Higher. Into a peak, where the face flashes, curls, caves. *BOOM.* A thunderous boom, breaking in slow motion, like an avalanche, frothing, misting, resetting the water.

To rise again.

"Hello, Mavericks," I say. The ocean seems otherworldly. Divine.

For a while, I lose myself. When thoughts return, the sun pierces a clouded veil, suggesting a gateway between here and everything. To my core, I'm certain, *There is so much more than we see.* In accordance, the waves thump. I'm awestruck by their enormity, and in their force, I see; I hear; I feel . . . eternity. Mavericks pulls me into a trance, which stays with me as I retrace the bluffs back to my car. Inside, I crank up the heat, the seat warmer, music. From a playlist, Jimi Hendrix covers Bob Dylan.

"All Along the Watchtower."

In tune with the lyrics, outside, the wind howls. My hair stands on end.

I return to the road.

58

FLOW.

Back in Venice, stories flow.

Whether real or imagined, Mavericks unlocked something. In turn, life courses through me, leaving a trail of words. Pages upon pages. Poetic prose. Delicious, peak state prose. My favorite flavors of life, woven together, with romance, celebration, connection. And above all, beauty, the pages drip in beauty. My chosen perspective. Through writing, I answer life's call. The call given in Hollywood, running through sprinklers, to the Rolling Stones. "She's a Rainbow."

To strengthen my response, I take a mentor to lunch.

Henry Miller on Writing.

It's a sunny December day. On a patio, on Abbot Kinney Boulevard, I open the book from Big Sur. Graciously, the Gjelina staff tends to me, as I devour Mr. Miller's mind, eating crispy, wood-fired crust, topped with burrata, roasted cherry tomatoes, anchovies. The rich meal befits Henry Valentine, a man of sensuous tastes. And though gone, his words leave a legacy, a record of beliefs, many resembling my own. No longer alone, I gain another companion. A partner in perspective, who welcomes me to . . .

"The creative life! Ascension. Passing beyond oneself."

By way of guidelines:

"There are no 'facts'—there is only the fact that man, every man, everywhere in the world, is on his way to ordination. Some men take the long route and some take the short route. Every man is working out his destiny in his own way and nobody can be of help except by being kind, generous, and patient."

With regard to craft:

"Writing was not an 'escape,' a means of evading the everyday reality: on the contrary, it meant a still deeper plunge into the brackish pool—a plunge to the source where the waters were constantly being renewed, where there was perpetual movement and stir."

By the end of my meal, I sense a graduation from Thoreau's *Walden* to Miller's creative life. A new approach: not evading the everyday but elevating the everyday. A new metric for success:

"My life itself became a work of art."

I circle the phrase; it offers a precise, personal mission statement. Life as art. Art as life. I decide to incorporate . . . all of me: peace with passion, work with pleasure, simplicity with luxury, rest with action, retreat with engagement. The spiritual *and* the material. Bridging the duality.

With balance.

With intention.

A way of being.

Inspired, I close the book. *This is it*, my inner voice tells me.

Integrity.

59

BRUNCH.

For the holidays, in Alta Dena, hosted by Isla and Hawk. Overlooking L.A., we gather in an oak tree sanctuary, as Hawk's mom leads us in qigong. Breath. Movement. Energy.

Once relaxed, we burn sage, and we write what we wish to release on sheets of paper. Isla fills a wooden trough with water. She explains that we've written on dissolving paper, and one by one we stir away our words.

Gone.

Refreshed, we sit at a table handcrafted by Hawk. He makes exquisite furniture. Our crew is creative: photographers, musicians, actors, models, directors, more. Together, we celebrate the end of a year, to the sound of jazz, from a reconstructed phonograph.

With merriment, a plant-based feast. Turning left, I reunite with Wallace, hearing about her life on location. Madrid. Punk rock gourmands. Artisan jewelry. Rose-petal cocktails. Long days. Longer nights. Getaways to San Sebastián, on my recommendation. "The pinxtos," she enthuses, talking with her hands. In her excitement, I'm back, and soon, we're combining memories, strolling narrow streets, restaurant to restaurant, red wine in hand, grazing on small bites. Olives. Fish. Cheeses. Together, we remember charming locals, live music, and high-quality coastal life.

"Have you read *The Sun Also Rises*?" I ask.

"No." A salad is passed; Wallace fills her plate.

"Not yet," I say. I excuse myself from the table, and one phone call later, Ernest Hemingway is in the mail to Wallace, from Book Soup.

When I return to the table, I turn right; I thank Isla for the brunch.

"You're so very welcome." She kisses my cheek. "What's new?"

"My writing," I say. "I have no idea where it will take me, but I adore it."

"Thank you," Isla says.

"For what?"

"For reminding me to enjoy the process."

She raises her glass.

Wallace leans over. "What are we toasting?"

"Life," Isla says.

"All good things," I add.

We toast.

"Hear that, universe?" Wallace calls to the treetops, "All good things!"

I pull both women close. Joyful. Vibrant.

Alive.

"GRACE!"

I hear a voice outside.

"Grace!" The call continues. I look over my balcony.

"Nate!"

Below, he stands, with two friends, in the beam of his vintage Land Rover headlights. I wave; he leans into the car; the stereo blares. Peter Gabriel.

"In Your Eyes."

"Nate!"

Pleased, he announces, "We're taking you to a surf party."

Soon, I'm in the passenger seat, telling the guys, "This is wild. *Last night*, I rewatched *Say Anything*. Tonight, my own Peter Gabriel moment."

Nate nods with satisfaction. "See?"

The guys laugh.

He explains, "The idea came to me out of nowhere; they called me lame, but I rolled with it." I place my hand on Nate's shoulder. "You crushed it."

Up PCH we soar, wind in our hair, stars overhead.

Past security, we reach valet, where angels offer cranberry kombucha garnished with sprigs of rosemary. Sipping my super-drink, I walk a winding driveway lit by lanterns. Each step, music grows, and the driveway opens to a lawn, in concert, on a cliff above the moonlit Pacific. At the head of the lawn, two Christmas trees flank a garland-draped stage.

In full swing, a darling band jams. Surf rock.

From afar, I watch as the drummer grins; the singer shakes his dreads; and the guitarist backbends from amp to crowd. Throughout the set, I meet more of Nate's friends. Vibes on vibes. And to clapping hands, I finish my drink, when another angel appears. "Cookie?"

"Please."

I hand her my glass, then I bite into a green-iced surfboard, with sprinkles. Beside me, Nate whispers, "Let's go to the front. You're going to love the next guy." He takes my hand; he guides me through merriment during the changing of the bands. As we reach the stage, a pair of boots knocks across wood onto a rug. In silhouette, I see a man with an acoustic guitar. Alone, he takes a breath. In his pause, I palpitate.

Next, he strums an introduction. The stage lights brighten; I know the song; I know the man. Easton Wylde. Hair cut short. Hat removed. Easton Wylde. My mood spikes. He looks up; he closes his eyes; and after an extended introduction, he holds the party . . . captivated. It's a classic, covered with the sweetness of a new parent, in lullaby.

"White Christmas."

I think of my family, of our traditions, and on the second verse, from beachy Malibu skies, *snow*. Manmade snow. I hold my hands out; Easton asks the party to sing along. In unison, we carol. And when the song ends, waves of applause, shakas, whistles.

"Thank you." Easton's dimples appear.

A single tear escapes my right eye. Easton trades guitars; he plugs in a jet black Les Paul. Meanwhile, his band assembles, and on the click of drumsticks, we take off.

All set, Easton rips and riffs, robust chords, wah-wah climbs. At one point, I go barefoot, to feel the grass. When I do, Easton notices. With a glimmer, he crosses the stage; he meets my eyes; he takes his guitar to his teeth. My very own Jimi Hendrix. Entranced, I raise my hands overhead, and in my lace-up bodysuit, I dance.

Euphoric.

Time stretches; time stops; the set simmers, but instead of exiting,

Easton calls for the opening band. A joint encore. Two groups as one. Dual drum kits. Dual bassists. Four guitars. Two leaders. A wall, a wave, an army of sound. Having the time of their lives, the rockers play a magnificent coda. "White Christmas," revisited, revamped, jammed out ten, maybe twelve minutes, culminating with *more snow.*

A wonderland.

"Thank you," I whisper to Nate. "Thank you, thank you."

"With pleasure," he says.

Around us, the music escalates and evaporates, leaving a DJ, who spins Allah-Las. I replace my booties. I feel a hand on my back. *His* hand. Seamlessly, I turn into a hug. *His* hug.

"Grace."

"Easton."

"You haven't called . . ."

"And yet, you found me . . ."

We hug again. A long hug. A deep hug. For over twenty seconds . . .

That man rocks me.

61

"KEEP GOING."

His voice assures me over Bluetooth.

"You sure?"

"Keep going, love."

"OK."

The day after Malibu, Easton invited me to hang out. "A rehearsal, a few mates." And so, I drive to meet him, through the woods of Topanga Canyon, at dusk.

"I think I see the house!"

"Good!" he says. "I've tasked a noble escort."

"Thank you, Easton, see you soon!"

I park. We hang up. On the porch, a boy, bouncing a red balloon.

"Hello," I say, exiting my car.

"Hello!" The boy catches his balloon. "I'm in charge of you." He runs over.

"Thank you." I smile.

"Take my arm," he offers. "They're out back."

"What a gentleman."

"You can hold my balloon if you like."

"Thank you."

"Mum says I'm a good sharer."

"I agree."

We embark.

Arm in arm, we pass a garden of fruits, flowers, vegetables; we wind around a large, bronzed Buddha; we reach a studio. At the entry, the boy releases my arm, uses the full heft of his weight to pull open the door. He lets me in. He approaches a second, soundproofed door, which he pounds with both fists: *knock, knock-knock*. The muffle of music stops. Easton greets us, "Thank you, little man. Here's Grace."

After I'm announced, I return the boy's balloon.

"Have fun!" the boy says.

"Thank you."

Easton brings me into the studio. It's me. And a band. When Easton invited me to rehearsal, he made no mention of the group. Now, he introduces a super-group, legends who need no introduction. They're rehearsing for a benefit. And when we reach the last member, he winks. "I know Grace."

It's the Rock God, from Chateau.

"How are you?" I kiss his cheek. He smells of vetiver, and he laughs.

"Still here."

"I'm glad."

Easton brings me a barstool; I take a seat; the set resumes.

"This one's for Uncle Neil," Easton says.

The drummer counts the start; the group strums a cover. Delicate, iconic chords. Chords I cannot name, but chords I know by heart: *da da-di da . . . da-da di da . . . da da-di da . . . da-da di da . . .*

To the music, I sway. The chords continue. I pinch my leg. They're covering Neil Young.

"Harvest Moon."

Chills.

When the song finishes, I can't help but clap. The group laughs, and the set list continues, for an audience of one. While I listen, I survey the studio; it's appointed with tapestries, crystals, concert posters, and framed records in gold, platinum. It's a time capsule of sorts, linking tonight with the best of nights.

Many songs later, there's pounding on the door: *knock, knock-knock.* The band breaks; a woman appears with a birthday cake. At once, a song, "Happy Birthday." The bassist shakes his head, the woman insists, "Make a wish."

Around the bassist, children and grandchildren assemble, including the boy, who bounces his balloon. "I hope your wish comes true."

"It already has, little man." The bassist smiles. "I've been amply blessed, and tonight, playing these songs, with these guys, for a good cause . . ." He chokes up. "It's paradise."

"Ain't that the truth." The woman, his wife, pulls him into a kiss. There's enduring passion, and the group cheers. Next, we eat cake. As I bite into German chocolate, I realize I'm at the right party. For me. By all measures, this is a working birthday, and yet, the bassist couldn't be more pleased. I'm at the party where work is pleasure.

Life as art. Art as life.

I smile. I think of Henry Miller. I lick frosting from my fork. During my introspection, the Rock God approaches me. "Easton says you're on a journey."

I sense what he means, so I answer, "Yes."

"That comforts my soul."

"It does?"

"Indeed. That last election scared me. Has America lost its mind? Its heart?"

"No," I assure him.

"Hope you're right. You know, we really believe in that whole peace and love deal." He takes a sip of water. "Can't let it die with us."

"It won't," I insist. The bassist walks over. "Chin up. We felt this way about Nixon."

The Rock God folds his arms. "True."

"Even in our darkest hour, the beat went on. Think of the music, the art." The bassist pats the Rock God's back, "The suffering sparked creativity, change."

Deep talk ensues. This group is well-read, well-thought, kindhearted.

The bassist surmises that since the dawn of politics, leaders have served as mirrors. In them, we witness our humanity, both dark and light. The Rock God proposes a choice. We can react: regression, hatred, division. Or respond: evolution, compassion, unity. If we choose the latter, we rise. In fact, a controversial leader can accelerate progress. By forcing us to face our shadows, we see what to heal, what to change . . . for the better. As we do, life conspires in our favor.

"Pronoia." Easton places his hands on my shoulders.

"What?" I look up.

"It's the opposite of paranoia. It's the belief in a good world, supporting goodness."

The bassist looks at Easton. "George? You there?"

Easton shrugs at me. "George Harrison."

The Rock God claps his hands. "I swear I see him in Easton. Like his energy went . . . everywhere, you know? And sometimes, it visits through Easton."

The drummer tings a cymbal. "Hate to interrupt, lads, but it's time."

Back at his guitar, Easton strums "Here Comes the Sun." The Beatles.

Everyone laughs; everyone sings.

It's alright.

62

WINTER SOLSTICE.

At the beach, on the shortest day of the year.

"Ready?" Easton takes my hand.

"Ready." I squeeze his grasp; we run to the ocean.

"When you hit the water, laugh," he says.

"Laugh?" I start—the very word inducing his instruction.

"Yes," he says. "Calms the heart. Opens the lungs. Absorbs the shock."

And so, like madman, madwoman, we enter a wintery Pacific, laughing. Among wetsuits, my bare skin shivers. I'm in a high-cut one-piece. He's wearing skull-patterned trunks. Cold water rolls over my thighs, above my waist. Soon, there's a big wave. We let go; I dive down, through, and up again, hushed by natural force.

Reset.

Invigorated, I grin at Easton. "Success." My teeth chatter.

"Breathe," he says.

I inhale. The chattering stops.

"The calm is real," he says.

"It is."

"Enough?"

"Enough."

"Tacos?"

"Tacos."

We run back. Up the beach, he hugs me into an oversized towel. The sun is a melon ball, slipping away, and I feel like a child again.

Exhilarated.

After tacos, we tour Easton's house. In the master bath, an antique claw-foot tub.

"Stunning." I run my hand along its edge.

"I should use it more."

"I would use it all the time." I think of Wes, Trey.

"Be my guest," he says.

"A bath sounds nice."

"Let me see what I have." He looks for supplies, then he prepares the tub. "Make yourself at home." He sets out towels; he leaves the bathroom; I slip in.

Through the door, I hear him brainstorming, a lick. New notes, over and over, finding their way into song. A break. He stops. Next, I hear a gentle: *knock knock-knock*.

"When you're done, I have a gift," he says.

"Bring it in?" I suggest.

"Your wish is my command," he says; I hear his smile.

The door creaks open. I settle beneath a blanket of bubbles. Sweetly, Easton writes my name on the fogged mirror before pulling a chair beside the tub. From his back pocket, he presents my gift, "From the Rock God." As I process the gift, he sits. It's a royal blue booklet, worn around the edges, no larger than his hand.

Steps Toward Inner Peace: PEACE PILGRIM.

Easton taps the cover. "When you left rehearsal, I shared your walking meditations with the guys." He searches his mind for my mantra, "*Om mani padme hum.*"

"Yes!" I cheer.

Easton's dimples return. "In response, the Rock God opened his guitar case. 'Everything for a reason.'"

My hair stands on end.

"He wanted you to have this."

Goose bumps cover my dewy skin. "Why?"

Easton offers context; he describes how Peace Pilgrim walked thousands of miles, crisscrossing the United States as a prayer for peace. To do so, she dropped her given name, adopting the name Peace Pilgrim. From her soul, she believed that when enough people found inner peace, the world would know peace. With each step, she spread her message, by example.

My shoulders roll back. "I'm not alone."

"Hardly." Easton replenishes my hot water. "It gets better. The Rock God received this booklet from Peace herself. Years ago. And he's carried it with him on every tour. Now, he's passing the torch." I smile. Easton smiles. "Shall I read a bit?"

"Please."

To start, an underlined passage, chosen by the Rock God, for me.

"All of us can work for peace. We can work right where we are, right within ourselves, because the more peace we have within our own lives, the more we can reflect into the outer situation."

From there, Easton flips at random, landing on steps:

> *"Simplification of life;*
> *Purification of body;*
> *Purification of mind;*
> *Purification of desire and motive;*
> *Relinquishment of attachments;*
> *Relinquishment of separateness; and*
> *Relinquishment of negative feelings."*

"Sounds like Franklin's Virtues," I note.

"All roads," Easton says.

He flips again. Though Peace Pilgrim is gone, as he reads, it's as if she's here. Her words extend her reach.

"My life is full and good, but not overcrowded, and I do my work easily and joyously. I feel beauty all around me and I see beauty in everyone I meet—for I see God in everything. I recognize the laws which govern this universe, and I find harmony through gladly and joyously obeying them. I recognize my part in the Life Pattern, and I find harmony through gladly and joyously living it. I recognize my oneness with mankind and my oneness with God. My happiness overflows in loving and giving toward everyone and everything . . ."

His voice pauses. Solemnly, he asks, "Remember when you asked about fame? It's simple, really."

He stands; he places my gift on the chair; he lowers his sweatpants, slightly, to reveal the Adonis belt of his abdomen. There, a tattoo that I never noticed: *I ask nobody to follow me.*

He sits down. "Gandhi. I wear it on my body to remind me of my purpose." He recites the full line, "I ask nobody to follow me. Everyone should follow his own inner voice."

I play with bubbles in my hands.

I look back at Easton. "Peace."

"She found you."

My heart fills. How lovely to hear peace personified in the feminine.

I decide to stay the night. In bed, I ask, "Tell me a story?"

"About what?"

"You."

He plays with my hair. "I studied Jurisprudence at Oxford."

"I had no idea."

"Few do." He laughs. "The day before graduation, I spent time in a record shop. There, I found a dusty album; it flipped a switch."

He didn't mention the album name. I didn't ask. Some things are meant to stay private. He did describe the album's impact. At once, he abandoned law, for music.

"What did people say?" I ask.

"Who cares?"

Who cares? So what. I think of Lance, of Page. I see boldness as a buy-in for passion.

"I wasn't listening to them," Easton adds. "I was listening to myself."

His inner voice. Easton believes it's his soul, the purest part of him that remains connected to all. Always. Source. How does he distinguish this voice among his thoughts? "It's kind." He smiles. "It champions my truth." By staying true, he escaped the herd; he individuated, moving from external to internal validation.

"Liberation," he says.

I sit up. "Freedom and love."

"Yes," he agrees. "Both are richer with peace."

I relax; we lie face to face; he explains the peace of creativity. Making something from nothing. Tapping into a higher consciousness. What he finds there, he turns into song. The process allows him to transcend himself. His explanation reminds me of the Rock God, of

Henry Miller. This life's not exclusive, but inclusive, for all who are open.

"It's better than an orgasm," he jokes.

"No," I mock-gasp.

"Well . . . the music lasts longer." He laughs.

"Easton?"

"Yes, love."

"I'm doing more than walking meditations."

"Are you?"

"I'm writing. Stories. They're flowing out of me."

"Your stream of consciousness," he relates.

"I guess so."

"Do you like Jack Kerouac?"

"I don't know."

He climbs from bed. "Let's find out."

Across the room, he starts a record that crackles into piano. When he returns, he turns off the bedside lamp. In darkness, over piano, spoken word.

Last I remember, Jack Kerouac, accompanied by Steve Allen, puts me to sleep.

"In some cases
The moon is you
In any case
The moon."

63

"COFFEE?"

He asks, early morning.

"Yes." I stretch in curtain-filtered daylight.

Out of bed, Easton replaces Kerouac with Chet Baker. To gentle tenor crooning, I dress. I've forgotten my sunglasses, so Easton lends me a pair of Persols.

"Queen of Cool," he jokes.

Up the block, visions of Steve McQueen dance through my head. On that vibe, we reach Menotti's. "Easton, Grace," the barista greets us, "your usual?"

"Yes."

We take our coffees to go, in the tumblers Easton brought from home. Arms linked, we stroll away from the VENICE sign, toward the beach, slowly sipping ourselves awake. Across the boardwalk, I veer left, our feet swishing wet grass. Leading our way, I approach the curved stone wall.

The Poet's Monument.

Silent, I stare at purple flowers, which lay, deliberately, at the foot of a poem.

"Zion," Easton says.

"What?"

"Who." He looks at me. "My best mate, Zion, you met him in Malibu."

"Blond, big smile?"

"Exactly."

I read the poem.

> *"Now the soft parade*
> *has soon begun.*
> *Cool pools*
> *from a tired land*
> *sink now*
> *in the peace of evening."*

"Jim Morrison."

"Yes. This poem's about Sunset," he says.

"Where we met." I lay my head on his shoulder.

A moment.

A breeze.

"Why the flowers?" I ask.

"Swell must have hit. Zion surfs big waves."

"Like Mavericks?" I light up.

"Just like Mavericks." He matches my enthusiasm. "The flowers pay homage to the waves."

"Tell me more."

Born and raised in Hawaii, Zion honors the historic tradition of blessing waves with prayer, offerings. For Zion, it helps him stay connected to the ocean, to earth, to all.

"How beautiful." I sigh.

"It is . . ." Easton looks away. "And speaking of traditions." He walks me to the Mark di Suvero sculpture. "It's called *Declaration*," he says when we reach the top of a grassy knoll. Beneath palm trees and sixty-foot-tall art, he brushes his hair back. "I declare my intentions here. Would you like to set one?"

"Absolutely," I say.

His dimples arrive. He tells me to close my eyes and give thanks. A brief, genuine thanks for my intention . . . already done. "Think it," he says, "and *feel* it."

I place my hand on my heart.

I'm there.

To finish, we walk the Venice Pier, as the sky releases rare drops of L.A. rain. On their touch, I remove the Persols; I lift my face to soft gray. At a leisurely pace, we reach the pier's end. Through the clouds, a few rays of persistent sunlight invoke the sense of heaven above.

"I leave for Park City tomorrow," I say. "By the time I'm back, you'll be gone."

"Only on tour. Not for good."

"True."

"Grace," he comforts me, "I'm never far."

I know this to be real. Still, I can't look him in the eyes. Instead, I stare into the ocean. "Thank goodness I found you." The water starts to sparkle; Easton moves behind me, and he holds me in his arms. "I found you." There's a silence. My stomach softens, and gently, Easton sings. It's almost a whisper, into my ear, an affectionate cover of Eric Clapton.

"Change the World."

For love, for truth, I smile, and Easton pulls me close. Our breath syncs. In the intimacy, I feel comforted; I feel secure. And though I enjoy Easton, my mind assures me that I don't need him. *I am whole, complete, as I am.* Without worry, I cherish the moment. And once again . . .

That man rocks me.

64

OLYMPIC VIBRATIONS.

On Christmas Eve, my ski boots clomp past a plaque. It reads: *Park City Mountain. Olympic Vibrations.* A nod to the 2002 Winter Games. I remove my mittens; I unzip my jumpsuit; I send a photo to Lance. "Puts me in the mind of you. Merry Christmas. xx G."

In Bondi, he's a day ahead. In Bondi, it's Christmas.

Time travel complete, I replace my mittens; I clomp out of the lodge for snowy weather. One more run. A final final before festivities. Loyal leads. Then, me. Then, Dad. Through groomed powder, we weave in and out of Aspen pine. At a landing, Loyal carves to a halt. "G,"—he points a ski pole to the sky—"your rainbow. Snow-bow?"

I join him, raising both poles overhead. "Yes!"

Earlier, I imagined a rainbow in the snow, for I couldn't help but think it would be beautiful. Curious, I asked our gondola, "Does such a thing exist?" Collectively, the group decided, "No," but Loyal tempered their verdict, "Never say never." One hot chocolate later, a snow-bow.

A halo, no less, encircling the sun. Loyal, Dad, and I remove our goggles to stare up the mountain, at a glittery snow-globe effect. Soon, our wonder starts a romantic rubbernecking. Skiers. Snowboarders. Teachers. Ski patrol. All slowing, stopping, in admiration. Beside me, a patrol says, "Isn't it mystical?"

"You took the words out of my mouth." I turn with a smile.

His cheeks are rosy. He's wearing red. His stubble is white.

"Santa?" I joke, though he's sexy and distinguished.

"Merry Christmas." His voice plays the part. He's made my day.

"Merry Christmas."

He skis away.

Snow-bow in mind, I finish our run, down the mountain, over the bridge, into town. Tussling my helmet hair, I de-ski and don a black trucker's hat. Deus Ex Machina. A coffee / motorcycle shop. Also, a literary device, God from machine, where an unforeseen event swoops in . . . resolving everything.

By our ski locker, I sit for the sheer bliss of unbinding my feet from ski boots. My toes breathe; my toes warm, and I lace up Sorel boots for après ski. Inside the bar, tinsel and bulbs decorate an enormous antler chandelier. From a high-top, Mom and Dechen wave, beneath a Christmas-light-wound Harley. Shaking off the cold, we hug. Then, I snap a moto-photo for Moses. "Happy Holidays! xx G."

Beers. Nachos. I head to the bathroom, checking my phone.

From Moses: "Awww Grace. Same to you, doll. Much love."

From Lance, a photo with Hemi, shirtless, cocktails raised: "Cheers! The Bunny."

Since yesterday, my messages read like a highlight reel, 2012–2016. Touched, I zip my phone away; I rejoin my family. Across the table,

Dechen's diamond ring sparkles. With Loyal, she recaps the proposal for Mom and Dad, who love the story.

We raise our glasses; then, a man approaches. "Excuse me."

When I face him, he confirms, "It's you."

I place a hand to my heart. "Have we met?"

"No, but I see you walking through Venice . . . in that hat."

"You're kidding." I stand. "I'm Grace."

Respectfully, my family meets our guest. First, my parents, "Genevieve and Charles." Followed by, "Dechen and Loyal."

"Jim," the man says. "I'm an Army veteran from Park City, but I've been in Venice, at the VA Medical Center."

Dad, also an Army man, extends his hand. "Thank you for your service."

"Well, sir, I'm here to thank your daughter."

"I see," Dad engages.

"I was in a dark spell, so my wife and son visited me in Venice. At the beach, my four-year-old noticed Grace. 'Daddy, she's doing PT.'"

Jim turns to me. "From that day on, I'd see you around town, running, walking, smiling, doing your thing. That pushed me. 'If she can do it, I can do it.'" He removes his hat. "And I did. I'm home for Christmas, Grace."

"Merry Christmas," I say.

"Merry Christmas," he wishes us well.

In his wake, our table is stunned. Dad chokes up. "Grace, this peace stuff of yours . . ."

He doesn't know how to finish, so Mom does.

"It's working."

65

TCHAIKOVSKY.

Christmas morning starts with classical music. *The Nutcracker*. I smell quiche baking. Holiday coffee brewing. My bare feet rise to heated floors. Outside, snow piles on the terrace, a white Christmas. With a stretch, I step into shearling slippers, and I walk downstairs to the great room to join my family.

"Merry Christmas!"

Two-story windows showcase winter, pouring down. By the tree, a pile of gifts, wrapped in our family tartan paper. Above a crackling fire, hand-knit stockings, in red and green, trimmed with white and gold. In the kitchen, Mom serves cinnamon coffee cake. A family recipe. Loyal dons a Santa hat, then he distributes our gifts, one at a time, from oldest to youngest in age. Around and around we go, little things, funny things, with meaning, sentiment.

Near the end, I unwrap a book. *Aspects of the Novel* by E. M. Forster. It's dated, but pristine, and there's a yellow bookmark. In wine letters: Borders Book Shop, Ann Arbor.

"The original Borders," Mom says. "According to the receipt, I bought that book in the seventies, but I never read it."

Dad chimes in, "I found it in the attic; I was looking for your mom's Phi Beta Kappa key, and there, beneath the miniskirts, sorority photos, and Michigan memorabilia, this book."

Mom insists, "It must be for you."

Among our family, Mom is most spiritual. Raised Lutheran. Presbyterian by marriage. A professor at Georgetown (Jesuit). For her, denomination never mattered; faith reigned supreme. When I was little, she gifted me a guardian angel. "Grace, it's important to believe in something. We're Christian, but it doesn't have to be Christ. I consider Jesus a wonderful role model, but he's not the only one. God is greater than religion."

Somehow, I'd lost my connection to God; however, sparked by divorce, I forged a new relationship, one that I feel strongly in this gift, this morning. Overwhelmed, I hug Mom; I hug Dad; then, I thumb through Forster's words, landing on a line I'll never forget.

"Human beings have their great chance in the novel."

I move the bookmark to that page. More encouragement, my path. And as if reading my thoughts, Dechen plucks a petal from a poinsettia. "Here, place it in the book."

"Thank you."

"This way, you'll remember this morning."

I add the white flower to the bookmark; I hug Forster to my chest. I know my way forward.

A novel.

66

VELVET RIBBON.

Our last night in Park City, on Dad's desk, I notice a stack of letters tied with velvet ribbon.

"What are these?" I call out.

"My letters from West Point and the Army," he says.

"When your grandmother passed away, we found them in her closet," Mom adds.

"May I read them?"

"Not sure they're interesting," Dad says, "but go ahead."

Permission granted, I sit by the fire, opening envelopes that explore Dad's past. By the dates, he wrote home every Sunday, without fail. And while the context was military, the reports were civilian. A Led Zeppelin album. Chocolate cake. Dinner with a family friend. Rounds of golf. Upbeat. Encouraging. Until a letter dated near his birthday, June, the summer after graduation. In place of his usual two typewritten pages, one handwritten line.

"What do you say about a boy being sent to war?"

My heart skips. Dad never mentioned Vietnam. According to his narrative, the Army sent him to law school; he joined the Judge Advocate General's Corps; he retired for private practice. Case closed.

I refold the harrowing page. I move to the next letter. It's dated three weeks later; two typewritten pages, a standard, optimistic report until the end.

"*By now, you must have received my previous letter. I apologize for the worry.*"

My eyes water; an explanation ensues.

"*When I last wrote I'd been called to Vietnam. Though I prepared for it, in some ways you're never prepared. After accepting my fate, the oddest thing happened, a mistake. As it turns out, I'm not being called to Vietnam. The orders were wrong. In the fall, I'm going to law school.*

"*As you know, I applied to Harvard, with encouragement from the Dean. However, West Point forgot to send my transcript. Rather than reapply, I've decided on Duke.*

"*Send my best to younger brother and sister. I expect to be home before school starts. Perhaps we can get in an afternoon at the club. It would be nice to have everyone together.*

"*Yours, Charles.*"

Carefully, I take both letters to my family. They're in the kitchen, having a political discussion.

"Dad, why didn't you mention Vietnam?"

Their discourse halts.

I hand over the letters; Dad skims them. "Because I never went."

"Yes . . . but . . ."

"No need to dwell."

"What happened in those three weeks?"

"I controlled what I could; I let the rest go."

Dad passes the letters back. A smoking gun. Proof that he practices as he preaches. I take the letters to his desk. When I return, Dad wraps his arm around Mom. "No Vietnam. No Harvard. On to Duke, where I met this law student."

The mood lightens.

"Movie?" Mom suggests. Dechen makes popcorn, and we head for the home theater.

"Grace?" Dad waits at the top of the stairs.

"Yes."

"You know I'm a big believer in positive thinking."

I nod.

He places his hand on my shoulder. "I get that these past few years have been challenging, but you're on a spiritual path, an artist's path, and I think that's cool. Your mom agrees, and we want you to know . . . we're on your team. If you need any help. Any financial support. We're here. For as long as it takes, we're here."

I burst into tears.

Relief from a burden that I didn't know I carried.

He hugs me. "Do what you love, Grace. Mom and I billed those hours, so you can do what you love. Consider us your patrons."

"Thank you," I whimper, my tears on his ski sweater.

"Keep your head up," he says.

I dry my eyes.

"And keep smiling." He rubs my back. "At the very least, people will wonder what you're up to." I laugh.

"We love you." He becomes serious.

"Unconditionally."

67

DAY OF THE DOORS.

January 4, 2017, a day designated to honor Jim Morrison, Ray Manzarek, Robby Krieger, John Densmore.

The Doors.

On my walk, I admire the band's name, added to the VENICE sign. I think of my electric shaman. I snap a photo, and, crossing the street, I think of *The Doors of Perception* by Aldous Huxley. I'd never read the book, but from the title, my mind moves to William Blake.

"If the doors of perception were cleansed everything would appear to man as it is, infinite."

The thought soothes me. I carry on.

Up Abbot Kinney, I am drawn to the mystical bookstore. I enter through the crystals. By the register, a calendar presents a spalike menu of services: tarot, aura cleansing, clairvoyance, astrology, numerology. The works.

To the scent of palo santo, I peruse a wall of books, finding . . . Huxley. In bright yellow and green, *The Doors of Perception*. From thought to purchase, with ease, in the flow of my morning.

Back home, I shower; I dress; I read the book—cover to cover, sans mescaline, a second-hand trip. Of particular interest, Huxley cites another philosopher, Dr. C. D. Broad.

"The function of the brain and nervous system and sense organs is in the main eliminative not productive. Each person is at each moment capable of remembering all that has ever happened to him and of perceiving everything that is happening everywhere in the universe. The function of the brain and nervous system is to protect us from being overwhelmed and confused by this mass of largely useless and irrelevant knowledge, by shutting out most of what we should otherwise perceive or remember at any moment, and leaving only that very small and special selection which is likely to be practically useful."

I flash back to Mavericks, to my thought: *There is so much more than we see.*

Building on Broad, Huxley suggests, *"Each one of us is potentially Mind at Large."* Huxley used mescaline to open himself up to revelations. During that time, he deduced that *sensitives* could experience ongoing revelation. Tuning in for hours. Days. Drug-free.

Ongoing revelation. How that entices me. If managed well, my sensitivity could provide an access point to infinity. Awareness. Knowing. With that promise, I decide to pursue meaning on my own, without psychedelics. For now. In my mind, it makes sense that we're automatically wired for connection. Certainly, surrogates may help, but why not explore innate opportunities. This way, I can tune in reguarly.

Any time, any place.

68

INAUGURATION.

Division. Fear. Tension.

Having stoked my sensitivity, I experience the unrest, acutely.

I'm pained.

Deprived of appetite, I force down a green juice. Loyal messages a quotation. Kurt Vonnegut.

"I was perplexed as to what the usefulness of any of the arts . . . The most positive notion I could come up with was what I call the canary-in-the-coal-mine theory of the arts. This theory argues that artists are useful to society because they are so sensitive. They are supersensitive. They keel over like canaries . . . long before more robust types realize that any danger is there."

I reflect.

Keel over?

"No, thank you," I decide. And from decision, resolution, *Roses. Like Wes, roses.*

Immediately, I move to action; I call a nearby flower shop. By sunset, I'm surrounded by fragrant white roses and candles. It relaxes my space. It restores my appetite. Calmed, I order a heart-shaped pizza, and for dessert, a documentary. *Bed Peace.* I couldn't control everyone, but I could control my own response. From John Lennon, I gain resolve.

"Peace, peace, peace, peace, peace, peace, peace. Peace in your mind. Peace on earth. Peace at work. Peace at home.

"Peace in the world."

Not a platitude, not a balm, but a focus.

A perspective.

A priority.

DETERMINATION.

Growing.

On my fridge, I leave myself a new note, Ernest Hemingway.

"I knew I must write a novel."

70

THEN CAME VALENTINE'S.

Sweet Valentine's, a sunny day, and the beach smells of sunscreen. In the quiet of morning, little stirs. Suddenly, up the Boardwalk, a young transient slams his possessions to the pavement.

"Because!" he shouts. "There's only now."

At his outburst, I slow my pace. In truth, he seems a bit off, but he seems a bit on. As he flickers in and out, I smile at him, sensing stress, not malice.

"You hear me?" he asks.

"I do."

"Thank God," he says. He picks up his crate. "Take care."

All is well.

The sand is groomed.

My beach run resembles a giant Zen garden.

I sprint.

I reach the break; it's buzzing with local surfers. As I watch, the lifeguards cruise up in their red truck. "Happy Valentine's, Happy Grace," their nickname for me, a testament to them, and their own happy state.

I near the ocean. Its waves crest higher than normal, exciting the long-boarders, who lift me, gift me a contact high. I remove my running shoes and socks; I wade into the water. Then, I crave Jimi Hendrix, so I shuffle on a playlist.

"Here He Comes (Lover Man)."

My feet sink into sand; waves lap against me. It's soothing. It's sensual. I close my eyes. I take a breath. I open my eyes. I exhale. When the song finishes, I wade back, where a surfer approaches me, his arms filled with flowers. Without a word, he hands me a red rose; he nods; he continues.

"Happy Valentine's," I say.

Rose in hand, I linger on my Love Street, reading purple letters on a white sheet, draped across a bungalow.

WHEN THE POWER OF LOVE OVERCOMES THE LOVE OF POWER THE WORLD WILL KNOW PEACE.

JIMI HENDRIX

From my AirPods, Hendrix sings, "The Wind Cries Mary." I brush the branches of an olive tree; I wonder about Mary. At the corner; I search the name's symbolism.

Beloved. Rebelliousness.

Yes.

On my way to Abbot Kinney, I take a side street. There, I notice the Neighborhood Book Drop, a wooden box, on a wooden spike, where books come and go freely. Lost in music, my arms act on autopilot, opening the glass door, when my eyes bring me back. A purple spine, two books from the right.

Jimi Hendrix. *Starting at Zero.*

Though Hendrix tempts me, I adhere to my rituals. I meditate, shower, dress, write. It's my path to ordination, my standing date with the muses.

My novel, unfolding.

When I hit my pages, I take myself on a date. Between the trees on Melrose Place, I enter a boutique, and in the sultry dressing room, I indulge.

I reclaim my sexiness.

For years, I wore lingerie for lovers. Now, for myself. An aesthetic practice. An act of self-love, honoring my entire humanity, which includes sensuality, sexuality, femininity, personality. In my experience, the right lingerie elevates me—to art. According to my own tastes. My own pleasures.

More than delicates, the pieces anchor a mindset, a reverence for higher sex, in service of higher love. Sex that exalts, creates, unites, transforms. Sex replete with possibility. Great sex. Satisfaction in the act. Satisfaction beyond.

Passion

Intimacy

Orgasm

Ecstasy

Divinity

Bliss

Balance

Creativity

Connection.

Swirling with insight, I stand tall, staring at myself in the mirror. Neither hubris nor humiliation, but power. And so, I reclaim my sexiness. I transform this holiday into a reminder to be mine. Always. Wrapped in luxury, I give thanks for how far I've come. I place my hands on my hips, and I tell myself, "I love you."

After dinner, self-pleasure.

In bed, in new lingerie, I open *Starting at Zero*.

Around me, candles burn. Sandalwood. Musk. With devotion, I pore over a compilation of letters and journal entries, glimpses into the man who made the music. I expect to read myself to sleep, but the pages keep turning with resonance. Many of Hendrix's thoughts could be my own. What a gift. On Valentine's Day, a lover man, in song, in book, a new rock angel. An ally. I'm comforted, and candles burning low, I mark two passages.

"People base things too much on what they see, and not on what they feel.

K. E. GREGG

"There's no bad people or good people; it's actually all lost and found. That's what it all boils down to. There's a lot of lost people around, and there are a few chosen people that are here to help get these people out of this certain sleepiness that they are in."

All along, people have roused me. They woke me from my sleep. For that, I am eternally grateful. To demonstrate appreciation, I can rouse others. *How?* Not through force or judgment. With love, like Hendrix. With art. With peace. With presence.

Arousal.

Breath fills me, and clear of mind, I close the book; I reach for my journal. There, I set an intention for my novel, for my future, using Hendrix's words.

"I want to turn the world on."

71

MARCH ROARS IN.

I've been writing, writing, writing.

One year since New York, since my wish for peace, for purpose. This morning, my eyes open to Lionel Richie, the Commodores, "Easy." To the song's alarm, I wake up; I dance on my bed, wishing myself "Happy birthday." No more faking it; I've embraced authenticity. At thirty-six, I am grateful, relieved.

Next, I enjoy my rituals. Making my bed. Stretching. Water with lemon. Meditation. Running. PT beneath the palm trees. A kiss to

Jim Morrison's mural. Menotti's, coffee. A walk through town. *Om mani padme hum.* Shower. Dress. Write.

Complete.

Then, by my mood, I drive up PCH to the Malibu Pier, where I watch the waves, the surfers, from an outdoor table at a café. It's simple, tranquil . . . and out of nowhere . . . there's a miracle.

It happens over pancakes.

First bite, I taste everything that went into my meal, my day, my life. All the people, all the energy, all the actions, all the elements that make me possible. As Peace Pilgrim described, I taste a "wonderful mountaintop," where my illusions dissolve into love. It's all love.

Over pancakes.

What a transformative moment, as honest as hilarious. Alone, in California sunshine, I am remembering. I get it. Call "it" what you will. A name is but a name. God. The Universe. Consciousness. All. As Alan Watts says, "You can't get wet from the word 'water.'" Words merely point the way, as best they can. Experience is instruction. And this experience, this pancake moment, is beyond. Beyond beyond, and I'm talking about a taste.

A mere taste.

Oneness.

K. E. GREGG

Where does one go from oneness?

I pay the check; I drive home; I return to my birthday. F. Scott Fitzgerald. *Tender is the Night*. Wishes from family, friends. A ceremony, where I review thirty-five, list what I want to release, and burn the page.

Next, a fresh journal. Envisioning thirty-six.

Finally, tea on my balcony, staring at stars. *I feel it*. Deeper pleasure. An everyday that feels like a holiday, where I require little and savor lots.

On that thought, my phone rings.

"Alexander." My voice warms.

"Not out?" he asks.

"In, having tea with the stars."

"What a difference a year makes."

"You wouldn't believe. How are you, Mr. DJ?"

"I'm in L.A."

"I'd love to see you."

"What are you doing tomorrow night?"

"No plans."

"I'm your plans. Pick you up at eight."

"Can't wait."

He nearly hangs up, but adds a thought.

"Wear sequins."

72

BACK IN BLACK.

Both he and I. At my door, Alexander, suited up, no tie, Stan Smiths. Meanwhile, I shimmer in mini-sequins, my Bondi sequins, with a leather jacket draped on my shoulders.

He has a car, from the host. A Tesla Model X.

On the ride to Bel Air, he reveals he's fresh off a ten-day Vipassana, a silent retreat. He does them regularly, to prolong his profession. When centered, he's able to swim in excess without drowning. At forty years old, Alexander prefers his nightlife in the role of observer.

"Key takeaway?" I ask.

"Equanimity."

In shared silence, we reach a gate, security. "I have the DJ." A walkie-talkie beeps. The gate swings back; our car lurches up the private drive. At the house, well-cast models brandish silver trays. Some offer, "Tequila?" Others, "Donuts?"

Politely, we decline the shot, but accept the chaser. Following a rainbow of lights, we walk red, orange, yellow, green, blue, indigo, violet, into the backyard. I polish off my donut, licking glaze from my fingertips. Then, my eyes feast. Mermaids and mermen, seducing a pool. A massive ice luge, carved as a unicorn, ten horns. "A decacorn," Alexander tells me. Nearby, a Champagne tower. Golden, bubbling coupes. For good measure, a few kegs, pumped by burlesque dancers to live jazz.

"Whose party is this?" I ask.

"Tech start-up," he explains, revealing what the Founder founded. At the name, I understand. "We're in his imagination."

"You're right." Alexander laughs.

"Wild."

Grateful for my sequined briefs, I follow Alexander across a mirrored dance floor. Simultaneously, we look up. There's a net.

"Ninety-nine red balloons," he says.

"Into it." I gear up for debauchery.

On the other side of the dance floor, Alexander helps me into the DJ booth, perched above partygoers. As Alexander sets up, I stare out, catching the smile of a young man in a hoodie and jeans. He's rapidly approaching, with a briefcase handcuffed to his wrist. When he arrives, his face lights up. "Alexander. Grace."

"You know my name," I reply.

"Always do my research," he says.

The Founder.

"What's in the briefcase?" I ask.

"Oh, this? I've always wanted a handcuffed briefcase. Between friends, it's not locked."

He laughs to himself, then he clicks open the case, revealing his wares. "Molly, edibles, joints, shrooms, ketamine, LSD, a few strands of cocaine."

"You really went for it," I compliment his bounty.

"Only turn twenty-five once." He closes the case. "I don't even do drugs, but people love drugs."

"They sure do," Alexander laughs.

"Anything catch your eye?" the Founder offers.

"We're good, man, thank you." Alexander smiles, then, he nods to a group near the booth. "They look down."

"Indeed they do." The Founder shakes his case, ready to make a move.

Before he goes, I ask, "Where can I find water?"

"Get excited." He points to a yurt. "There's a water sommelier."

"Of course there is! Happy birthday! Thank you for having me."

"Thank you for being here." The Founder blushes.

He's off.

One water-tasting later, I return with still, sparkling, domestic, foreign. Triumphant, I present the selection to Alexander, when he spots a friend. "Lou!"

As he waves to her, he tells me, "My actor friend, you'll love her."

Soon, Lou reaches the booth, she's wearing a blazer, no shirt, no bra, bolo tie. Her blond hair cascades down her shoulders, and she's carrying a vintage Hermès clutch.

"Grace, Lou, Lou, Grace," Alexander says.

When we hug, Lou says, "I think we wear the same perfume." Shrouded in mock secrecy, we whisper the scent to each other.

"Yes!" Lou says.

"I feel like I've known you . . ." I start.

"Forever," Lou finishes my sentence.

Alexander's set begins.

Fast friends, Lou and I celebrate until a dancer pops out of a cake. Confetti guns. Photos. Then, Alexander spins Nena, the original version, in German.

"99 Luftballons."

The red balloons drop.

"Life." Lou laughs, wonder in her eyes. Her clutch vibrates; she excuses herself to answer her phone. When she returns, a question, "Karaoke?"

I turn to Alexander. He's finished his set; the live band has resumed. "I have to spin again at dawn," he answers. "It'll be weird then. Go karaoke."

"You sure?"

"Absolutely. We'll catch up tomorrow."

Big hugs, and we're off, through the party to Lou's car service. Out of Bel Air, we ride, making conversation. Not small talk, real talk.

"Alex tells me you're a writer."

"I am."

"Anything I know?"

"Not yet," I say.

"Art takes time." She smiles. "Do you know how long I acted before my first role?"

"How long?"

"Seven years. I call them my lucky seven."

"Why?"

"They taught me patience."

"Thank you."

"Of course. Why did you become a writer?"

She swivels toward me, with interest, attention. In response, I weave highlights from Sydney to present day. Afterward, she places her hand on my arm.

"Your Hero's Journey."

The space inside my chest grows, cools. "Like the Odyssey?" I ask.

"Yes."

I let that sink in; she continues, "It's a thing, for all of us. I researched it for an audition. We're all on a journey, with trials, and triumphs, and transformation. If you look closely, in every darkness, there's a spark. It's on us to fan the flames."

She glosses her lips; I make a note in my iPhone; our car enters a vacant lot, a lot that would be supremely sketchy apart from an impeccably suited man. "Welcome!" Lou exclaims to me, as she rolls down her window, greeting the man, "Owen!"

"Lou, Grace." He opens the car door, "Lovely to see you."

When we slide out, Lou whispers, "I gave him your name, and I'll connect you by text. This way, you can come anytime."

"How thoughtful," I say, touched by her generosity of spirit. Through the emptiness, my stilettos meet the grit of asphalt, following Owen, Lou, to a deserted mini-mall. Down the escalator, we pass darkened shops, heading into a service hallway, which leads to a velvet rope, a bouncer, double doors. With Owen, we gain access. There's a massive aquarium in the entry, then a trail of soft blue lights. These lights guide our path through a gauntlet of suites, each ringing with long-lost hits. At the end, we reach No. 9.

A red door.

And through that door, delight.

Late-night karaoke.

I enter a group of friends, at the height of excess. The room is mirrored, adding to the drama of a smoke machine and disco ball.

Beneath spinning lights, three women share two microphones, singing a seductive Bob Dylan.

"Lay, Lady, Lay."

I remove my jacket. Once exposed, my sequins come alive. Around the room, Lou introduces me to faces from movies, TV. Person by person, I sense a bond. Apart from the fame, there's a common kindness. Most notably, among the women. Like Lou, they embrace me. One offers to store my jacket. Another orders me sparkling water. A third passes the songbook.

No two alike.

All beautiful, in their own way.

Not a mean girl in the house.

Over the course of late night, I witness a spectrum of adventure. Some sober. Some drinking. A touch of weed. A few lines. To each their own. Nobody harshing anyone's mellow or high. As refreshing as inviting, it was a confident, good time. And underground, the hours disappear in song, cuing a flash of the lights.

"Last call?" I ask Lou.

"Last song."

"The usual?" someone asks.

"Yes!" the group decides.

A circle forms; Lou pulls me in. Together, we follow lyrics, which scroll across a tropical beach. The woman on my right tells me, "They added this song for Lou."

It's Ohia. "Farewell Transmission."

My first time hearing it; my first time singing it. As it happens, it's the perfect song. The lyrics re-anchor my soul, my guidance.

Listen.

73

ICE CREAM.

In Venice. Honey lavender. Walking up Abbot Kinney, we lick ice cream cones, talking about last night. At one point, Alexander stops. "The goose is out."

"What?" I stop.

"It's a puzzle, a koan. I read it in Osho. Today, it feels like your goose is out."

"Alexander. I sense you're being soulful . . . but it sounds dirty."

"Fair enough." He laughs.

We resume walking; I link Alexander's arm. "Now, I have to know."

"Well . . . to me, it seems like things are coming together for you—less force, less worry."

"I agree." I savor purple ice cream. I appreciate his perspective.

We cross the street; Alexander reaches for his iPhone, where he finds a bookmarked passage. He reads aloud, "If a man puts a gosling in a bottle and feeds him until he's full-grown, how can the man get the goose out without killing him or breaking the bottle?"

I stop walking; my brain ignites, off to the races for resolution. We move to the edge of the sidewalk. While I churn, Alexander reaches for my hand, and passionately, he kisses it.

I'm stunned, out of thought.

He notices; he kisses my hand again. "The goose is out."

Technically, he could have clapped or shouted my name. To startle. Instead, he chose a touch of romance. Equally unexpected. Memorable. In his kiss, the bottle no longer existed, thereby, freeing the goose. "The goose is out," I say. Happy.

We resume walking; Alexander explains how a koan can't be solved, only *dissolved*, leaving the conflict for the present. Far from logic, I understand. Since moving to the beach, I treated life like a puzzle. To that, Alexander asks, "What if there's nothing to solve? Nothing to fix? Only moments to live."

"Choices," I say, recalling my original intention on that Echo Park sofa.

"Yes."

Alexander illustrates his point with examples. The tech party. Karaoke. Both proved valid meditations, fostering mindfulness, seizing my awareness. *Here. Now.* In hindsight, I see that I gave my full attention to celebration. No ghosts from my past, no pull from my future. No diagnosing life. No dimming life. Instead, diving in. Fully.

Living.

Next, he discusses the mechanics of mindfulness. "You're using a point of reference to pull you from thought to focus. It doesn't have to be isolation or deprivation; it can be pleasure."

He's so open that I relay my pancake moment, the oneness over the ocean. He hugs me.

"I've felt something similar in Vipassana."

"Really?"

"Really. When you're focused out of thought, you reconnect with the stillness, the vastness, the God within."

"*Yes,*" is all I can say.

He laughs. "Where'd you feel it?"

I place my hand on my heart. "Here, then everywhere."

My diaphragm softens, tuning back to Malibu. Those pancakes. That state. "I wish it lasted longer," I say.

"It's a practice," he says, "but you know that."

"I do."

"I've got a vibe for you," he says.

And via text, I receive an album.

Moby.

74

SUNRISE, MEDITATION.

I listen to the album from Alexander, Moby's *Long Ambients 1: Calm. Sleep*. There, I access a pocket of stillness. Out of stillness, I receive a calm thought: *Thank you.*

Refreshed, inspired, I write.

Mid-morning, I take my run to the Venice Breakwater, where I notice two words written in the wet sand.

THANK YOU.

75

CHANCE.

By chance, I happen upon the Rock God's gift while searching for a necklace, in my keepsakes drawer.

Pleased, I remove the book; I fasten my necklace, then I flip the book open at random. My eyes catch words; they nudge me from study to action. Embodiment. In those words, Peace Pilgrim describes a turning point: "*So I got busy on a very interesting project. This was to live all the good things I believed in.*"

"Mmmm . . ." I nod. She's right.

I place the book by my bed.

Her turning point triggers mine.

76

PINK TIGHTS.

Black leotard, canvas slippers, legwarmers, messy bun. Years since my Hollywood class, I return to ballet; a friend of a friend teaches on the Westside.

Tuesday morning, I enter her studio. Wooden barres. A wall of mirrors. A piano. A touch of sweat. Dancers, aged twenty-something to seventy-something, chat while they stretch. At ten o'clock, the pianist plays a scale up the keys; our teacher enters. "Good morning, I am Eleftheria."

She's Greek.

In Athens, I met another Eleftheria, with Maxime. The name means "freedom." The name has me smiling. I'm in the right place.

"To the barre," Eleftheria says. We awaken our feet. Afterward, she welcomes us. "This class is for you. It's not competitive; it's for love."

My first-class jitters subside.

From pliés to grand battement, I move to Eleftheria's instruction. On tendu, she asks us to picture our toes dragging through sand. On rond de jambe, she encourages the "painting of watercolors." During adagio, she notes, "Everything is of equal measure, it's up to you to find balance." Across the floor, she asks us to feel the light, radiating from our core.

It's poetry.

With every combination, my energy rises. I cherish fundamental steps in new patterns. It's a powerful class, one that unlocks peaceful passion. In the end, I'm happy to show appreciation. Révérence.

First, we mark the steps. Then, the pianist sits back; Eleftheria plays a song from the stereo. Leonard Cohen. "Hallelujah." Only, she doesn't start in the beginning, she starts near the end. As I dance, my mind suggests, *Forgiveness.*

Hallelujah, hallelujah.

No specific person, no specific harm. A blanket forgiveness, shedding the weight of being wronged, doing wrong. I'm not unpacking it. I'm not condoning it. I'm releasing it. As I dance, I'm moving on. In this révérence, I forgive others; I forgive myself.

Tears in my eyes, clear of mind, I receive new thoughts: *I am enough. I am loved.* When class ends, I thank Eleftheria. "I feel restored."

Hallelujah.

77

RAIN.

After forgiveness, a storm.

To falling water, I remember people, connections. Friends, lovers, on my path, off my path, over years of change. Some stayed; however, many cycled in, out, seasonal, situational, come, gone. I miss them. I think of them fondly. I've been blessed by a steady stream of support, apart from one limitation—my clinging. Craving stability, I attempted to hold onto people . . . long after they were meant to go. In those instances, I suffered. In those instances, I tainted beauty with futile attempts at control. Where I come from, you could count on connections for a lifetime. Where I am now, anything could happen. Rather than lament this reality, I decide to get curious. I ask myself, "Why?"

My mind answers, *Growth.*

There's a break in the rain; I take a walk. On Abbot Kinney, fresh street art. Not fancy, but formidable. In black script on a white wall.

Someone loves you.

The art inspires two thoughts: *I am enough. I am loved.* Soon, I find my steps syncing to these thoughts, all the way to the Neighborhood Book Drop. Stepping across the reflection of palm trees in a large puddle, I open the glass door to see what's available. A car passes; water whooshes; I notice a title: *The Essential Rumi*, translations by Coleman Barks.

I remove the book. It's been read, well-read, and as I hold it in my hands, I know I'm supposed to take it home.

It's here, for me.

Before reading, I take a bath. Candlelit. With bubbles, lavender, Himalayan sea salts. Self-soothed, I take Rumi to bed, to freshly laundered sheets. Under the soft glow of an Edison bulb, I turn to a random page, as is my process, with my higher self. On that page, poetry speaks to my earlier inquiry.

> *"You moan, 'She left me. He left me.'*
> *Twenty more will come."*

I place the book on my lap. Rumi reminds me to stay open, to trust my path. Over the beach, rain resumes; thunder, lightning. Divinely timed, the storm feels like a cleansing.

"Twenty more will come," I say, as I turn out the light. "OK."

I follow my breath.

I sleep.

78

THANK YOU.

On wet sand, by the break, I use my foot to trace words.

THANK YOU.

Standing by my message, I thank my soul for guiding me, and I stare at the frothy Pacific. *More will come.*

I inhale deeply.

I head to town.

As I walk, I appreciate Venice, observing every detail with the eyes of a lover. Flowers. Sunshine. Shops. Homes. Another display of street art. Larger. Bolder.

Someone loves you.

I approach the wall; I underline the message with my fingers, when I hear a skateboard. It sounds fast, but as it reaches me, time slows. I turn.

"Grace." He stops.

"Yes?" I'm trying to place him.

"Zion, Easton's friend."

"Valentine's." It clicks. "You gave me a rose."

"I did."

"Thank you."

"Admiring the wall?"

"I am."

"You're such a beach person."

"I am, but why do you say so?"

"Head held high, enjoying your day, not on your phone."

"I wasn't always this way . . ."

"You are today." He nods. "Buy you coffee?"

"I'd like that."

And then, there were two. Zion, in high-tops, cropped linen pants, a hoodie. "Ready?" he asks me. "Let's go," I say. In response, he pushes his foot into the tail of his skateboard; he picks it up, and he carries it by its side. Like that, we stroll. He's wearing a giant smile, which he extends to all who pass.

It's who he is.

Taking our coffees to go, we wander back to the beach. There, I follow Zion toward the water. In the last bit of soft sand, he buries the nose of his skateboard. Beside it, we sit.

"How big are the waves you surf?" I ask as we watch surfers on longboards.

"Well,"—he looks out—"the waves here hit three, four, maybe five feet."

"OK."

"My record is fifty."

"*Fifty feet?*"

"Fifty feet."

His chest rises; his smile grows. "The dream is seventy-five."

That's a seven-story building. He tells me a wave that big moves near fifty miles per hour.

"How would that feel?" I think out loud.

"Humbling," he says.

He says it firmly; he says it with respect. As he sips his cappuccino, I sense no bravado, only love.

"Does it scare you?" I ask.

"Sure." He twists his silver rings. "But fear is my starting point. It informs me. It activates me." He laughs. "It's not going anywhere, so I've made it my friend."

I smile; I sip my coffee.

As we talk, Zion can't describe a single ride. Typically, when he pops up, he goes blank. No mind. Luckily, sponsors film him. That said, without evidence, he would do it for the high. "When I close my eyes," and he does, "I can drop into the feeling," and he does. So much so, that I tune into his mood.

With Zion, I return.

Oneness.

He finishes his coffee; he's quite philosophical. "The body craves predictability," he says, "but the soul thrives on expansion." Coolly, he articulates his view of God. "I believe we're all part of one consciousness, divided into unique beings, meant to be diverse, as a means of expressing, experiencing . . . infinity."

I nod.

"By following my dreams, I honor my life, my God. The totality."

I nod.

"Did you always feel this way?" I ask.

"I spend a lot of time alone, in the ocean, waiting on waves. I suppose that's where it occurred to me."

He explains how he watches the world, looking for swell, opportunity. He explains, six, eight-hour stints in the water, hoping. He details his training: clean eating, seldom drinking, no drugs, hydration, sleep, running, swimming, yoga, breath work, meditation. Then, he lists his equipment, including brightly colored guns, as he calls his ten-foot boards, plus safety vests, with ripcords that release carbon dioxide, pulling him up.

"From the abyss," he says.

Silence.

"We've hardly explored the ocean," he adds. "How far does it go?"

"Maybe it's infinite," I connect.

"Totally." He admires the water, with tenderness. "The ocean is my biggest teacher. Look how it moves. In and out. Change and renewal. Each wave is one of a kind. Each wave is part of the whole. Nothing's permanent. It's all fluid. Unpredictable. Mysterious. You can't control it, but if you're ready, you just might merge . . . with perfection."

My spine straightens.

The sun hits the water. Glistening.

"It's like heaven," I say.

"It's *everything*," he answers.

We're calm, yet engaged, talking without trying.

"We're in flow," Zion says.

"But it's not extreme," I answer. "I associate flow with extreme action, intensity."

"Trust me," he says. "There are countless access points."

"I'm for it."

"Smooth mind, smooth ride." He laughs.

Silence.

"Do you visualize?" I ask.

"Not like other athletes," he says. "Tough to rehearse an unknown wave. But . . . I do put myself in the ending."

"The ending?"

"My happy ending,"—he laughs—"back on shore, after that seventy-five-foot wave, spraying Champagne."

His calm peaks with ecstasy. I feel it. I join him.

"Go there often?" I ask.

"Sure. I mean, the whole point is the feeling, right? Why wait?"

"Great call." I memorize his high.

"It's my ideal," he says, "and it fuels my choices. People ask about discipline, but really, I'm aligning with that seventy-five-foot wave. From there, each step becomes essential. For me. For life. By showing up, I demonstrate my commitment."

"Get ready; stay ready." I say.

"Yep." He laughs. "It works. Life wants to flow through us. So, I stay focused, open."

"Best of both worlds."

"Particle and wave."

"You lost me."

"It's a bit heady," he confesses. "I'm on a quantum kick."

"Quantum?"

"Quantum physics, quantum particles . . . the little things.

Protons. Electrons."

"Got it."

"I'm on airplanes, often; I use the downtime to learn."

"Why not dabble in quantum physics?"

He laughs.

"What excites you about particles?" I ask.

"Lately, it's the double-slit experiment. When observed, a photon . . ."

"Light?"

"Yep." He's stoked. "When observed, a photon collapses into a particle, meaning it's in one place, defined. But if no one's watching, data shows the photon as a *wave*. In a state of potential. *Everywhere* at once."

"That *is* heady," I say. "If particles behave that way, and particles make up you, me . . ."

"Exactly. I think *life* behaves that way."

"Making anything possible."

"Making *everything* possible."

"Depending on our focus . . ."

"Yep," he says. "And *that's* what excites me."

My eyes water; I admire the surfers.

"You're like a guardian," I say. "On the threshold of infinity."

"Spoken like a writer." He laughs. "If I'm a guardian, I'm the benevolent kind. Not kicking people out, but inviting people in. Cool?"

"Cool."

A wave crashes. Zion places his hand on my shoulder.

"Welcome to the party."

79

FOCUS.

All summer, I focus.

Come September, I revel in creation. First draft of my novel, complete.

As I print the draft, my phone rings; it's an invitation from Lou. She has an extra ticket to Tom Petty and the Heartbreakers.

"In."

Monday morning, we check into the Hollywood Roosevelt, turning a show into a staycation. Walking into the hotel, my iPhone buzzes, photos of Isla and Hawk's baby boy. All around me, creativity is happening, in its many varied ways.

Life.

Flowing.

I take the room keys. Lou tells the concierge, "We're celebrating."

"What's the occasion?" he asks.

"She finished a novel," Lou says.

"First draft," I clarify.

"Well on your way." The concierge smiles. "A milestone."

Upstairs, we enter a hallway decorated with Slim Aarons. Photography. The collection sets the tone for leisure, and soon, we reach our cabana room. On the mirror, in red lipstick, I write a line from Rumi.

"May the beauty we love be what we do."

After a day at the pool, we return. There, beneath Rumi, a bottle of Champagne, on ice. The note reads, "Congratulations on the novel." It's signed by the concierge, Francis. From prep school, I remember St. Francis's prayer—peace to all beings. I take a breath; I pop the bottle. Lou opens her bag. "I knew these would come in handy."

"Cheetos?" I ask

"Champagne with Cheetos." She smiles. "I dated a sommelier who swears by this pairing."

She rips open the bag.

We put on robes.

For sunset, we relax on the balcony, with our Champagne and Cheetos. Below us, the DJ spins a chill, dancy version of "Harvest Moon." It's

Poolside, covering Neil Young. Meanwhile, the sky dazzles us with violet cascading into pink, adorned by palm tree silhouettes. We clink our flutes; there's a knock at the door. Pizza. Pepperoni and jalapeño.

We wine; we dine; we dress for the show.

Outside the hotel, we're on Hollywood Boulevard. The Walk of Fame. Lou stomps her foot. "Grace." It's the star for the Doors. Lou takes out her iPhone; she plays the Doors.

"Break on Through."

Pleased, I step onto the star; I think of Jim Morrison, electric shaman.

"When you step forward," she says, "you're entering a new reality."

Ignited, I dance forward. To the other side. In turn, we laugh; we walk through stormtroopers, Obi-Wan Kenobi, Luke Skywalker, a range of impersonators. It's Monday night, not too hectic, so we enjoy a walk, uphill, outpacing cars to our destination.

The Hollywood Bowl.

Right on time, we reach our seats, in a garden box. It's my first Tom Petty and the Heartbreakers show. With humor, Lou whispers, "You always remember your first."

It's the last night, a bonus night, of the 40th Anniversary Tour. Around us, the amphitheater percolates. The Bowl brightens; the Bowl dims, then, Tom Petty appears, with the Heartbreakers.

"He looks like an angel," I say.

"A rock angel," Lou agrees.

The show begins.

Hit begets hit. Tom Petty shares stories, memories, photos. From time to time, he gushes, "Thank you. Thank you. I love you. I love you." By "Breakdown," I'm floating. It's a clear night, and the crowd sings along. As we do, it feels like summer camp.

The set goes on. During "Wildflowers," I'm especially moved. To the music, I gain a sense of belonging. Feeling free. Among the free. Later, "Runnin' Down a Dream." Fully present, I align with determination, creativity. In that moment, I recall wisdom from Tom Petty, that music is magic. It moves us. It speaks to us. From that thought, an intuition: *Music guides us through the mystery.*

As for this music, this night, it's the ultimate sound healing. I bet Nate would agree. I've been happier than happy, from beginning to end. When the band exits, I remain standing, with Lou, with the entire Bowl, in united iPhone ovation. Our light demonstrates awe, admiration. In response, the band returns.

Encore.

"American Girl."

At ease, I dance, gazing up at the large cross, glowing, on a hilltop beyond the Bowl. Finally, Tom Petty bids us "Good night," and I gain this overwhelming sense . . .

Rock and roll heaven.

On earth.

80

STRIKE.

After the show, Spare Room.

We enter to the sound of bowling pins, falling, from the edge of the cocktail lounge. Still buzzing on music, Lou and I wait by the bar. A creak. A wooden wall opens, revealing a hidden photo booth. Out of the booth steps an exotic woman, trailed by a younger man, fawning over his photo strip. She kisses his cheeks; he blushes. "Thank you."

"She's an actor, from Paris," Lou whispers, as the woman strolls toward us, to the bar. She's elegant, magnetic, and despite the strictly nonsmoking situation, she opens a silver case lined with impeccably rolled joints. "You mind?" she asks us, as a formality, before lighting up.

"Not at all." Lou smiles. "I'm an actor; I love your work."

"Thank you," the Parisienne says, leaving no trace of lipstick as she takes a few small hits. At the smoke, the bartender gives her a look. "OK, OK," she says, extinguishing her joint. "Champagne?"

Ice broken, we have a drink together, making conversation, mostly about movies, until the Parisienne asks me, "What do you do?"

I hesitate.

Lou intervenes, "Grace is a writer." Then, she specifies, "A *novelist.*"

I pull my shoulders back. It sounds right. It sounds real. I'm quite pleased. I'm having a moment . . . when I'm bumped. An influencer, filming herself, knocks my glass from my hand, and oblivious, she carries on. The Champagne splashes my bare legs, before the coupe shatters on the floor. It's a scene, but with the wave of her hand, the Parisienne elevates the scene. "Baptism by Champagne!"

"Yes!" I rub the bubbles into my skin.

"A novelist," she says. "With legs for days."

We laugh.

The bar back comes over. "Are you OK?" He's a gentle giant, and he's concerned. "I am, thank you." I look him in the eyes. He cleans the mess, and the bartender brings a fresh fizzing glass. "For the novelist."

The Parisienne winks. Lou cheers. I feel their care, their support, and this glass tastes sweeter. Next, I ask the Parisienne, "Would you tell us about the seventies?"

"Did we miss the party?" Lou wonders.

"You know . . ." the Parisienne pouts, "We just *lived*, like you two. Whenever you are alive, *that* is your party."

She shares a few stories. This club, that yacht. A taste of her era, paired with a warning, "It flies." Her eyes dart to the door, they widen. "That's my guy." Her husband approaches. "I'm ready to take you to bed," she tells him. "Isn't he sexy?"

He laughs; he pays our tab; we exchange good-byes.

"Make the most of it," the Parisienne says, departing. And for clarity, she looks back, over her shoulder.

"*Life.*"

81

SPLASH.

I dive into the saltwater pool. It's early. I have the hotel to myself. Back and forth, I swim, in silence, until, "Grace." By the pool, Lou waves good-bye; she has a meeting with her agent. In the morning sun, I float. Then, I plunge, submerging myself entirely. Everything's hushed. When I return to the surface, I feel renewed. I climb the ladder; I towel off; I return to the room.

Breakfast.

Showered, dressed, I sit on the balcony for waffles with berries, whipped cream. As company, *Albert Camus: Notebooks 1935–1942.* Another mentor. Before opening the book, I recite a Camus line that I love, "The world is beautiful, and this is everything."

I fill my mug with black coffee, then I flip to the bookmark. Sipping, smiling, I read,

"Being able to live alone in one room in Paris for a year teaches a man more than a hundred literary salons and forty years' experience of 'Parisian life.' It is a hard, terrible, and sometimes agonizing experience, and always on the verge of madness. But, by being close to such a fate, a man's quality must either become hardened and tempered—or perish."

I reflect.

Solitude, as an accelerator. My instincts were right. My Walden taught me plenty. Fortunately, the time hadn't hardened me; it made me more compassionate, more open. In solitude, I learned my optimal state. Of course, my environment helped. The beach. But this morning, as I bite into waffle and strawberry, in Hollywood, I have that beach feeling. In many ways, it's a feminine feeling. Receptive. Responsive. At ease. In flow. Now, I carry the beach with me.

As I write.

As I live.

As I am.

82

"TOM PETTY."

Lou calls one week later. "Grace, Tom Petty died."

I'm speechless. A few tears commence; I apologize.

"We're artists," she says. "We feel deeply."

"I appreciate your condolences over a man I never met."

"He touched your heart," she says.

"He did. I can't believe he's gone."

"It flies," Lou quotes the Parisienne.

"Make the most of it," I follow. "On stage, he looked so fulfilled. Didn't he?"

"He did. I'm certain he got his wings," she says.

"A rock angel." I smile.

After our call, I crave music, so I choose Tom Petty's other band, the Traveling Wilburys.

"End of the Line."

I think of Tom Petty with George Harrison and Roy Orbison at what the Rock God calls "that concert in the sky." Later, I drive to the Tom Petty and the Heartbreakers star on Hollywood Boulevard. There's a crowd in vigil. Candles. Music. I place red roses on a pile of mementos; I blow a kiss.

"Thank you. Thank you. I love you. I love you."

83

BOLDLY INSPIRED.

I write.

For months, I write and rewrite.

Devotedly.

What's more, I approach art like an athlete. My intention? Mastery.

From high-performing humans, I have learned what helps. Now, application—turning knowledge into power.

I enhance my rituals. "Olympian mode," I tell Isla, Wallace, Lou, my family. With resounding support, my inner circle cheers me on. I'm also encouraged by Wes, Nate, Easton, Zion, my neighbors, my community.

Building momentum, I complete a second draft, a third draft, my performance improving. Moreover, my *voice*. It's starting to sound like me, feel like me. In effect, this novel is practice, training. I'm developing the means to express life's beauty. "You have an interesting perspective," Dad says. "Your job is to articulate that perspective as well as possible."

In the mail, Mom sends a card, a reminder from Edgar Degas, "Art is not what you see, but what you make others see."

Sharing.

On that mission, fall slips away. Come December, I skip festivities, save one, the holiday party at Sunset Marquis. *Go*, my inner voice suggests. *Go*. Compliant, I dress in velvet pants, a plunging top. Then, I call a car. As it happens, the driver is listening to Guns N' Roses.

"Want me to change the music?" he asks.

"No, I love it."

He adds volume.

We drive to West Hollywood. On the way, it starts raining.

At 1200 Alta Loma Road, I watch raindrops ping off the up-lit awning. Before I exit the car, a sexy Santa greets me with a large umbrella. Once inside, I thank her, and my stilettos click toward the glamorous sky-high Christmas tree. There, a bad Santa holds court with artists, rebels, the Stetson hats of Southern rockers. "Ma'am." One tips his brim, clearing a path for my passage.

"Thank you." I make my way to the courtyard, where clear tents cover pool and gardens. Staring up, I relish the tapping rainfall, and the DJ plays Patti Smith.

"Because the Night."

Warmly welcomed, I head for Jim Morrison's portrait, on display from the Morrison Hotel Gallery. While paying homage, I hear a woman over my shoulder, "He was a really lovely guy."

"You knew him?" I meet a vision, seventy, maybe seventy-five years young, with an understated cool that I wish I could bottle.

"Quite well," she says.

I lose my breath. My inner voice nudges, *Ask.*

"Would you describe him for me?"

She deliberates; then, she releases a single word, "Bemused."

"Bemused."

"Yes," she says. "And by that, I mean amused from within."

My smile grows; she offers more. "Even at his most famous, Jim would never run up and assert himself. Instead, he hung back; he looked you in the eyes; he drew you in."

"That's how I imagine him." My hands float to my heart.

The party fades away; the Sage continues, "Jim was so sensitive. Shy.

That's why he had to get blotto to go on stage. That's why he started with his back to the audience. In rehearsal, he sang facing his band-mates. It took a lot for him . . . to turn around."

She approaches the photograph. "Out of the spotlight, he was truly romantic; he cared for people. We'd go to these dive bars. He'd sit in the corner, and he'd buy drinks for people who had no idea who he was. Over drinks, he'd ask for their stories. That made him happiest, people and their stories."

"I'm the same way," I gasp.

"Poet souls." The Sage grins. "He would have liked you."

A few guests stumble near, reinserting the party into my reality. After they pass, the Sage extends an invitation. "Want to feed the koi?"

"Yes."

I follow her up a footbridge. There, she pulls a pill bottle from her purse. I start to wonder if "feed the koi" is a euphemism for drugs, when she sprinkles fish food into my hand. "Koi bring fortune and courage," she says. "Make a wish."

Slowly, I sprinkle the glassy pond, bringing a rush of gold to the sur-face. *May fortune and courage smile upon me.* At the end of my thought, the Sage says, "I have something for you. Let's go downstairs."

Away from the party, we walk to the hotel's recording studio. When we enter, there's a joyous welcome from the Sage's friends. Behind them, a mixing board blinks red and green. In the corner, she pulls a book, a pen, from a cardboard box. Around us, carols play; Bruce Springsteen sings "Santa Claus Is Comin' to Town." The Sage sits on a leather sofa. "What's your name, dear?"

"Grace."

"How fitting." She uncaps the pen. "Grace, Grace, Grace. What shall I write for Grace?"

She looks at me; she looks at the page; she begins thoughtful cursive, explaining, "Keith says peace and love, but the Dalai Lama says peace and happiness." As she speaks, she completes a hybrid-dedication: *"With love, to Grace, peace and happiness."*

I handle the book with care. It's a photo book. "Filled with Jim," the Sage says.

And that's how it happened, Jim Morrison, Keith Richards, and the Dalai Lama, blended together, in West Hollywood.

"Do you write?" the Sage asks.

"How did you . . ."

"Depth," she says. "Jim's heroes were writers."

My heart skips; after a delay, I recognize the Sage. She's a legend. In her eyes, she knows what's happened. In her eyes, she finds it endearing, and we hug. The hug could have lasted forever, but her assistant beckons.

"Someone to meet," the Sage apologies.

"I understand."

"Remember, Grace, if you have *faith*, you will *live* in the City of Peace and Happiness."

"Thank you." I hug the book to my chest.

"Merry Christmas."

84

A BAGPIPER.

In full Scottish regalia, three days before Christmas, on the sleepy end of the Venice Boardwalk.

Struck, I stop to hear him play. As he warms up, I am transported to the Scottish Highlands. To my family's heritage. Overhead, a prop plane. At the outdoor showers, surfers rinse away their morning session. In the wind, palm trees bend, rustle. The first song begins.

"Amazing Grace."

It's breathtaking. Soulful moaning, droning. For a second, I am tempted to take a video, but I abstain. I'd rather absorb every note he plays. I'm hyper-present, and when the song ends, I clap, filling his case with cash. "Merry Christmas."

I resume my run.

Chalked on the pavement, "You are loved. You are love." Around a bend, a neighbor walks his pit bull rescue, Huggy Bear. I pet Huggy hello, as my neighbor and I appreciate the crisp, sunny weather. I sprint away. Volunteers serve breakfast to the homeless. A local salon offers haircuts, shaves. At the sand, Alexander's tech friend, the Founder, spots me. He mutes his conference call. "Hello, my decacorn." I laugh; I sprint away.

On the beach, my local surf instructors. I blow kisses. They wave shakas. I rest. Near the water, two bright orange towels, a European couple on holiday. Despite the cold, she tans topless as he reads aloud from a book. I sprint. Along this stretch, I hear a beat, a pulse. Soon, a drummer comes into view. A teenager, with his kit in the sand, facing the ocean. I stop. I stay a while, and I picture my rock angels, looking down from above.

My heart expands.

I sprint.

I reach the break, where waves mix blue with white. A little boy digs himself into a life-sized hole. From the baby blue tower, a lifeguard waves. "Happy Grace!" Emphatically, I reciprocate. I sprint. I finish at my usual spot, tracing my daily message in the wet sand.

THANK YOU.

Beside my message, I take a breath; I fall in love. With the morning. The community. The beach. *Everything.*

Fully, in love.

Flying high, I finish my PT; I stroll to Menotti's. Through the entry, vinyl plays. Jay-Z, sampling the Doors.

"Takeover."

I remember Sydney, 2013, that sunset on the cliffs, with Lance. Nearly five years later, my new self is my truest self. Loving. Writing. Sharing peace. After Lance, I think of Wes, Trey, Vlad, B, Alexander, the Bad Boy, the Rock God, Maxime, Moses, Nate, Easton, Zion . . . all the men I admired, who honored me by returning me to myself.

Over the years, I deferred less and less to men, joining them as an equal. Moreover, I found women on the same frequency. Isla, Wallace, Lou, the Parisienne, the Sage. Out of my thoughts, I start a conversation with the barista, who wears a feminist pin on her apron. Preparing my order, she tells me: "The King commands, but the Queen demonstrates. As women, we lead by example. By our very being."

That clicks.

She treats my coffee.

Outside, I cue my iPhone. "Takeover." On repeat. Shoulders back, I walk to Jay-Z, Jim Morrison. At the corner, I wait for the light to change.

There's a tap on my shoulder.

"Ford?"

"Gracie!"

It's Ford, my sweet Ford, a nickname for the fourth in his lineage. Out of D.C., out of context—a surprise of incalculable measure. He's late for a meeting, so he quickly invites, "Tonight? Craig's?"

Instantly, I know my answer, "Yes."

"Wonderful." He hugs me off my feet. "Seven-thirty," he says. "I'll be waiting outside."

"See you then."

85

MELROSE.

In West Hollywood, Ford waits outside the restaurant, all grown up. Far from Yale Lacrosse shorts, he wears short-hem pants, loafers without socks, and a suede jacket.

"Gracie, you look stunning," he says.

"Thank you."

As we enter Craig's, he gives me an update. "Dad and the guys are fifteen minutes away. Bar?"

"Bar."

Hand on my back, he ushers me through the festive happy-hour crowd. At a red barstool, he invites me to sit. "Champagne or martini?"

"Martini."

Two arrive. Dirty. Rocks glasses.

"Ford and Gracie ride again," he toasts. And despite the years, we're back to our bond. Effortlessly. Fifteen minutes pass in a snap. His phone rings. "Dad"; he excuses himself to take the call. He hands me his wallet, the wallet I've known forever, leather with a cross-stitched IV. I pull out his Platinum Amex, and I hand it to the bartender. While waiting to sign, I notice a book. The man on my left has an autobiography. "You're reading *Slash*!" I exclaim. The man laughs; he looks up; he's Batman. Out of the movies, into real life, Batman.

Through my excitement, I manage to say, "What a book."

"Have you read it?"

"I have. I have a thing for rock biographies."

We connect; we talk books, and I make my confession, "You're my favorite Batman."

"Am I?"

"You are, and now you're the Batman who likes Guns N' Roses. Even better." I bite an olive from my garnish, for emphasis. Batman laughs, and behind us, I hear a big, Southern "GRACIE."

"William!" I excuse myself, leaping to hug Ford's dad, a towering, retired U.S. senator.

"You remember these two?" He points his thumbs at two men.

"I do." I hug the congressmen. One Republican. One Democrat.

"This is Batman," I make the group's introduction, prompting Batman to ask, "Are you committed to calling me that?"

"I think so," I say. "After all, you're my favorite."

"You make a point," he jokes. "How could I refuse?"

"You can't." Ford laughs.

"No, sir," the Senator echoes.

Fast forward, the six of us have dinner in a booth, sipping Barolo, two insane bottles, from the Senator's collection. It's mostly shop talk, when the Senator asks, "Gracie, what's good in Venice Beach?"

"I'm writing a novel," I say.

"Hot damn." He claps his hands. He tells Batman, "Whip smart, this one, whip smart."

"Our secret weapon," one congressman says. The Republican.

"We tried to steal her," the other retorts. The Democrat.

"For what?" Batman asks.

"To run for office," the Senator says.

"What happened?"

All eyes on me, I don't politic or panic. No smoke. No spin. Instead, I speak truth to power, "Not my vibe."

"I see." Batman nods.

"I'm a lover, not a fighter. And now, I'm independent. I care about everyone."

"Big ole heart." The Senator grows sentimental and continues, "Ever since she was a little girl."

Feeling accepted, I share a story. A visit with UNICEF, where I asked a field worker, "If you had one wish for humanity, what would it be?" Instantly, the field worker moved her hands to prayer. "I wish we would remember that there's no us or them, only us."

I watch the Senator's eyes mist. He makes himself vulnerable. "If I had to start again, in this climate, I'm not sure I'd run."

Ford's jaw drops.

The Senator swirls his wine. "The older I get, the more I value happiness. Peace of mind. Hell, peace. I can't define it, yours is yours. Mine is mine. That's part of the deal, but if we can spread joy, calm, even a little bit, that's a win."

I raise my glass. "Let's drink to that."

Later, the Senator shows me a video of his oldest granddaughter's ballet recital. Our server pours more wine; Batman's phone buzzes. He looks at the phone; he winks at me. "That's my signal." To the others, "It's my assistant, my ride."

He stands, but before leaving, he asks for a pen. On command, the Senator unsheathes his Mont Blanc.

"Give it to Grace," Batman says. Next, he hands me his book. "Will you sign my *Slash*?"

"Stop it." I laugh.

"Not a chance," he insists.

So, I lean in, for my first book signing. Well, my name, Slash's book, but given my GNR love—it's a dream dress rehearsal. I flip my hair, and in fine fountain pen, I pass on the Sage's message:

"With love, to Batman, peace and happiness."

"Collector's item," he says. And to bipartisan cheers, he goes.

Once he's gone, I tell the group, "Thank you for accepting me as I am."

"Of course," the Senator says.

"Always," Ford echoes.

86

CHRISTMAS EVE.

I land in D.C.

Down the escalator, Frank Sinatra sings "The First Noel." At baggage claim, I hear Dad's voice. "There she is!"

I'm overcome. It's Dad, Mom, Loyal, and Dechen. "Surprise!"

It's been a year since I've seen them. The longest we've gone apart. I blink through happy tears, as we hug and laugh and hug. All the while, Sinatra sings.

Noel, Noel.

87

AT THE CLUB.

I run the treadmill; I shower; I meet Mom and Dad in the Grille, overlooking the golf course. At a distance, the Washington Monument.

"The last day of twenty seventeen," Dad remarks.

"And we're with Grace." Mom takes my hand.

We smile.

Amid holiday décor, we lunch. Like Dad, I order the Reuben sandwich. When we finish, my parents drive me from Army Navy to Belle Haven, to Kricket's, a friend since preschool ballet. On my arrival, the door to her colonial brick house opens. Kricket waves from the front steps, holding her golden retriever by the collar.

"Hi, Kricket!" Mom rolls open her window.

Dad helps me with my bag; he hugs me; I tell Mom and Dad I love them. Up the brick path, I reach Kricket, whose Cartier bracelets jingle as she envelops me in a hug.

"Grace!" Dad approaches. "You forgot something."

In his hands, a jeroboam of Champagne, the equivalent of four regular bottles.

"Charles saves the day!" Kricket laughs.

Dad hands over the gift, and like in high school, he tells us, "Have fun, be smart, be safe." He places his hand on my shoulder. "If you need me—"

"You're a phone call away," I finish his sentence.

With that, Kricket welcomes me home, her home.

An hour later, chocolate chip cookies in the kitchen, with Kricket, her husband, Grant, and their four-year-old, Finn. A scented candle burns. Kricket asks Alexa for Tom Petty.

"You remembered," I say. "Of course." She smiles. To the music, the doorbell rings.

"Hair and makeup," Grant answers the door. "Finn, let's go to the movies."

The guys depart; we transform from day to black tie.

"What are you wearing?" I ask Kricket.

"I'll show you," she says.

After running upstairs, she returns with two garment bags. Unzipping the first, she reveals a winter-white, one-shoulder dress.

"Stunning," I say.

"Thank goodness I'm tan."

"Palm Beach for the win."

Kricket laughs; she zips up the garment bag, and a bit coy, "You?"

"Nothing new."

"That's what you think." She presents the second garment bag. "Your friend Lou sent this, from her stylist."

"What? Did you look?"

"*Yes*," she says, with a tone that means *you'll love it*. Slowly, she lowers the zipper.

"Gold!" I cheer. "Sequins." I pull my hands to my face.

"*Balmain*," she says. "With briefs to match." She lifts up the mini dress. "Very you."

"The most me," I sigh. We laugh.

I FaceTime Lou.

"Thought you might want some alchemy," she answers.

"You're the best."

"*You're the best.* Have fun! Happy New Year!"

In his navy tux, Grant snaps photos of Kricket and me, by the mantle. Prom style. And true to that mood, a honk outside. Kricket grabs the jeroboam; Grant helps us with our furs, and we step into the cold, where I meet another surprise. "A party bus!"

"Like old times," Kricket says, as we mount steps into blinking lights.

"Gracie!" the bus welcomes me.

"Bunny!" a few add.

"She's back," Kricket says.

We take our seats. Grant unleashes three liters of Champagne. The bus departs. To stories and memories, we cross the Potomac River, from Virginia to a sparkling District. It's fun; it's festive, and as we did in our twenties, we make the rounds, visiting Lincoln, Jefferson, Washington, the White House, the Capitol. I feel nostalgic. I feel thrilled. It's the perfect pre-party en route to Georgetown.

"Too bad Ford couldn't make it," Grant says.

"I know," I agree.

"He's dating a sorority girl," Kricket updates me. Ford hadn't.

"We were in sororities," I say.

"No . . . she's *currently* in a sorority. She's a senior at GW."

"Get it, Ford," I laugh through my confusion. *Why didn't he tell me?*

"He's biding his time," Grant says.

"For what . . ." I start to question, when Kricket plays a song.

"Murder on the Dancefloor."

Sophie Ellis-Bextor. Our anthem. At once, we leap from our seats. I fill with years of happiness. We sing. We dance.

We arrive.

88

PRIVATE PARTY.

The sign says, on the second floor of the restaurant, a back room.

Private party. A great call for us. A great call for the other diners.

In our room, we're rowdy. Laughter, banter around a mahogany table. On my right, Kricket, Grant. On my left, another dear friend, Maggie, her husband, Mark. From there, five other couples. Since I've been gone, our group grew up. They've married, started families, risen through the ranks to law partners, lobbyists, consultants. Most impressive, the continued friendships, the joy, the refusal to succumb to stereotypes.

Politics is like drugs, like money. How you go in is how you come out.

More Champagne pops. Pappy van Winkle joins. The 15. Healthy pours open vaults of stories. Hard-hitting issues like, "Who's sent or received a dick pic?" The room squeals. Luckily for us, our wildest days occurred in the dawn of social media.

"No posts; no problems," Maggie jokes.

"I love you." I squeeze her tight.

"Awww, lovey. We miss you."

To eat, Kricket and I share one lobster, one bone-in ribeye. Our go-to, DIY, surf and turf. Over dinner, voices grow louder, echoing off the walls. Hours fly. Our bus returns.

We're off to the main event.

THE RITZ-CARLTON, GEORGETOWN.

After giving our names to the event planner, we climb the hotel steps. Up top, we're handed Champagne; we check our coats, and we brat-pack the step and repeat.

Through ballroom doors, a twelve-piece funk band wails, covering the Commodores.

"Brick House."

The scene is hypnotic, shimmering, silver and gold; with massive flower arrangements; chandeliers; and a canopy of balloons. There are party hats and noisemakers. Decadent, sweet treats. Multiple bars around a packed dance floor. Quickly, I recognize faces. It's a who's who from my past, from prep school to the Hill. I spot my first boyfriend. Another boyfriend. A mean girl. Maybe two. That guy, with his tie around his head. That wife, pretending it's funny. Most couples have young ones at home, but tonight, they're hall passing. Hard.

Near eleven, a dance circle forms. Wedding style. Amid revelry, I spot a few side eyes. My dress. It's short. It's flashy. It's incurring judgment. *Fuck it*, I think, *it's New Year's Eve.* Saving the day, Maggie pulls me into the circle, dancing with me, loving me, as I am. Soon, Kricket joins, and I remind myself, *Focus on the lovers*.

I let go.

More dancing, more drinks, and the lead singer prepares us, "Five minutes until midnight."

Guests start coupling up. At the edge of the ballroom, a few perpetual bachelors, available for one night, one night only.

"Three minutes until midnight."

I back away from the dance floor. Scanning the room, I feel aftershocks of my transformation—from head of the class to outlier, outsider. No date. No mate. No kiss. No plan.

Fuck me.

I flush. The walls are closing in. *Air, I need air.* A bit panicked, I escape. Without a word, I grab my coat; I run down the stairs. Past the doorman, I rush outside. It's freezing, but I inhale a deep breath of relief.

"OK," I say aloud, watching my breath hang in the night. *I'm spiraling into comparison. I can stop this.*

"Ten, nine, eight . . ."

I stomp my stiletto. *I love who I am.*

". . . Three, two, one."

"Happy New Year!"

I hear the ballroom's shouts and noisemakers. Alone, I lift my face to the sky. As I do, the Doors.

"Touch Me."

My ringtone.

An unknown caller . . . still, I answer, "Hello?" I recognize the voice; it's Easton's manager. "Grace, love, can you hear me?"

"I can!"

"Have a listen to your man."

It's Easton, playing "Auld Lang Syne," Hendrix style, as if christening my free mind. On the streets of Georgetown, I did it. I faced pain and chose peace; I returned to my path; I honored my path, even when overwhelmed.

Certainly, I knew I'd been changing; after all, the point was transformation. However, until this homecoming, this midnight, I never realized how much. I left a lot behind to grow into my future. It's natural to mourn, to grieve. It's OK. A bit lonely at midnight, but OK. For as I heard James Taylor explain, "A little loneliness grants a lot of freedom." That's where I'm headed. That's what I'm about.

Inside, I may have missed or ignored this call. Outside, I started the New Year with electric guitar. The sound of my soul.

"*Happy New Year*," I gush, at the song's end.

"I'll send you the recording, love, so you have it," Easton's manager good-byes.

A bundle of emotions, I debate whether to stay or go, when I hear a line.

"Of all the gin joints in all the world . . ."

It's not cringey; it's not cheesy, for one reason. The delivery. It's meant to make me laugh. It's Ford. He's walking up the street, in a wool coat over a white dinner jacket. Bow tie undone.

"Heard you had a sorority date," I say.

"Didn't work out." He grins.

"Why?"

He doesn't answer, but when he reaches me, I know. *I'm why.*

Nervous, I wish him, "Happy New Year."

"Happy New Year, Gracie."

2018 starts.

2018 freezes.

89

WE DRIVE.

Top down, past the Pentagon, past Arlington National Cemetery, over Memorial Bridge, from Virginia to D.C. It's January 3rd, and we're in Ford's grandfather's Mercedes, a Yale blue 1967 280 SL. Drivable art.

"Is this yours now?" I ask.

"It is. Granddad's humor . . ."

Indeed. Years ago, Ford "borrowed" the car, and enticed by spring, we skipped school to visit the cherry blossoms. Somehow, we managed airtight alibis. No lacrosse for him. No ballet for me. Overachievers unleashed.

That afternoon, we walked the pink, flowering Tidal Basin; then, we purchased Slurpees, which we took to the Lincoln Memorial. In the sun, we relaxed on legendary steps. If I close my eyes, I can still taste blue raspberry and see ripples in the Reflecting Pool. It would have been the perfect caper, but someone recognized the car. Ford's grandfather was a big deal in D.C. Bigger than we understood. One phone call, and we were busted. Well, not instantly. Ford's grandfather appreciated rebellion, so he let us enjoy ourselves, until . . . the next day. We were both grounded, but as I told Ford, "Worth it."

Many years later, the day lives on, in the form of an inheritance, a car bequeathed as an inside joke. Bravo, William II. Wind in my hair, I shout praises to Ford's grandfather, and in his honor, we play Arlo Guthrie.

"My Peace."

Recreating our memory, we veer right at the bronze horsemen, parking near a hot dog vendor. Through the grass, instead of Slurpees, we finish third wave coffee. Adulting. The Memorial is quiet, nearly empty. We climb the stairs, and at the top, we sit. For January, it's lovely. The tree line of the Mall is bare, but the weather is pleasant. It's fifty, fifty-five degrees and sunny. Nostalgic, I stare into the Reflecting Pool. Today, it's still. No ducks. No ripples. Only a pristine mirror image of the Washington Monument.

"Look at us now," Ford says.

"Wild ride." I laugh.

From there, we contrast teenage dreams with reality. For Ford, it lines up . . . to a T. Yale lacrosse, White House internship, Capitol Hill staffer, Virginia Law. Next, he worked his way to head of corporate affairs, finance, someplace fancy. His success earned him a Georgetown brownstone, world travel, summers in Nantucket, golf, ski, and the like. Before the age of forty, he had all the memberships, access, and perks one might imagine. Maybe more.

As for me, I went from good girl to gone. After starting my golden climb, I leapt, shedding prestige for an intro- spective tour. By the beach, far away from the haute-herd, I questioned . . . everything. This revealed the real me. Not much on paper (yet), but in-person, I feel grounded, calm, authentic.

"You're free," Ford says.

"I am." And because I feel safe, I swallow my pride. "Have I squan- dered privilege, though? Have I fucked this up?" I gesture to the city.

"Please." He looks at me, adapting a quip from his nickname-sake, Henry Ford. "Whether you think you fucked up or didn't fuck up, you're right."

That brings laughter.

"Seriously," he insists. "It's your call, but for what it's worth, I think you're turning privilege into peace. The world needs that."

"That's the dream," I say.

"Good." He stands. "Let's celebrate with lunch."

At once, I recognize the burgundy-painted brick.

Inside, it's a bit musty, but I swear I smell Santa Maria Novella. That cologne. That apothecary. Florence. My heart races; I scan the dining room. *Is he here? He's not.* I smile at the memory; I shake it off; I return to present company.

Sally greets us, "Hey, kids. How many you got?"

"Two," Ford says.

"Take your usual table." She gives me a hug. "Gracie, welcome home."

To the corner, we stroll a sea of white tablecloths, as Ford shakes hands. Behind him, I smile; I wave, in leather pants and a turtleneck. I'm far from conservative, but I feel fine.

With Ford, I always feel fine.

After working the room, we reach our table. Much like Ford's car, it's been passed down. William II, III, IV (Ford), all prefer the corner. Involved, yet slightly removed. We both order the crab and crab. One crab cake. One jumbo lump crab. Sally treats me to a glass of Champagne. Over bubbles, Ford and I trade stories, until he softens his tone.

"Gracie."

"Yes?"

"Why don't you move back? With me?"

I pause.

"We'd be great together. You know it. I know it. I'll fix you a study in my brownstone. You'll have access to Georgetown's library. You can spend time with your parents, Kricket, Maggie. You can drive the Mercedes."

"But Ford . . . I love L.A."

He hears me; he amends his offer, "Alright. We'll get a place there, too. By the beach. Or in Laurel Canyon. Midcentury modern. A rock feel. Whatever you want." He takes my hands.

"Would that work?" I ask.

"Absolutely." He leans closer; he hushes his words. "At least, until I run for office."

"That's new."

"What do you think?"

My heart sinks. "What about my wild side?"

He takes my hands. "Gracie, the world's changing."

"You say that . . ."

"I mean it. I promise. I'll take care of everything."

He would. Of that, I'm certain. And suddenly, I have a date, a mate, a plan.

He pulls my hands to his lips.

A kiss.

90

THE ARCHIVES.

700 Pennsylvania Avenue, NW.

A place to get away, to think. On my own, I stroll renovated halls; I visit the original signed Declaration of Independence. At first, I'm tempted to weigh the pros and cons of Ford's offer. Then, I relax.

I wait.

My answer will come.

After the Archives, I wander the neighborhood. I reach Warner Theater. At its sight, I clasp my mouth. The Washington Ballet. My dancing days, the *Nutcrackers*, the *Swan Lakes*. The tutus, the symphony, the anticipation in the wings. A magical time that lands in heaviness, heartache. I quit dancing to follow the pack. *Not again,* I decide.

Writing is my second chance.

I brace myself beneath the marquee; I call Ford.

"That was fast," he answers.

"Ford,"—I'm not questioning; I'm convinced—"your offer is beautiful, but I have to keep going. I can't turn back."

He goes quiet.

He returns, "I get it. And I want your happiness with or without me. I don't need to be with you to care about you."

I'm touched. "*Ford . . .*" I say his name; I have no other words.

"I mean it, Gracie. I do. If you need to keep going, keep going. Just remember, it's not your accomplishments that make you worthy of love. It's you."

"*Ford . . .*" I start to cry. He comforts me, "I know you don't want to hurt me. In fact, I think you're brave; I admire you. We're all doing our best. We're all trying to make the best of this life."

Relief.

Ford took nothing personally. He didn't make my decision about him; he listened to me. It wasn't moving in together. It wasn't a wedding announcement. It wasn't even dating. But it was there, and it was real. I felt it.

Love.

Going further, he articulates what many WASPs struggle to state.

"I love you, Grace." He uses my grown-up name.

"I love you, Ford."

Finally, he lightens the mood. "Read any good books lately?"

I'm laughing. My tears are gone.

The friendship remains.

91

GENTLE GRIEVING.

Mourning.

Though amicable, my decision with Ford compounds feelings from New Year's Eve. A loss of childhood fantasies. This holiday, I could have tied my life with a bow. A picture-perfect ending to my journey.

My ego would have been thrilled, but my soul has other plans: *Keep going.* And so, I pack my bags. One more night with my family, then L.A. The beach is calling.

Downstairs, I hear Dad's vinyl. Stéphane Grappelli. The sound signals wine hour. I zip up my luggage; I join them in the living room. When I enter, Mom stands. "Grace, come with me."

We walk to the kitchen, where two items lay on the island. "Your dad found these in the attic," she explains.

I hadn't mentioned Ford's offer. I hadn't mentioned the Washington Ballet. But in front of me, I find a box of pointe shoes. My final Chacotts, never used. Veronese II. Teary-eyed, I open the Freed of London box. I hold pink satin in my hands; I inhale the canvas lining.

Mom allows me a moment.

Next, she directs my attention to a book. It's leather-bound, with a title I don't recognize: *Fairy Tales from Many Lands*, edited by Dinah Craik.

"Open the cover," she encourages.

To Grace, for all the wonderful stories you've written in the second grade. Keep writing! We love you! Mom & Dad

"Second grade?" I ask.

"Yes."

"Keep writing?" I ask.

"Yes."

Dad calls from the living room; Mom hugs me, smelling of Estée Lauder Beautiful. Then, she leaves me to me. I sit to cheerful jazz violin. I think of Lance, of his question in Sydney, "What did you dream about as a child?"

Tonight, I remember.

Stories.

Part Four

92

GIRLS' NIGHT OUT.

Lou booked a role. *The* role.

To celebrate, dinner. A woman-owned restaurant in Koreatown. A menu that spans the globe. Compliments of the chef: mackerel toast, yellow corn ribs, beefsteak tomato. Then, Lou's favorite, the scallion, salsa negra, lime frog legs. During that course, we don't speak. We're all about the dish. Once it's cleared, Lou asks, "Have you heard of Hydra?"

"No."

"It's an island in Greece, Leonard Cohen lived there."

She searches for photos on her iPhone.

"Gorgeous," I admire the landscape.

"When my movie wraps, let's go," she says. "Imagine us on a boat . . . dancing."

"Done." My heart warms.

Across the table, Lou plays with her necklace, a mother-of-pearl caviar spoon on a chain. Up the handle, an engraving, *Amor Fati.* "Love of one's fate," she explains. This Stoic concept helps Lou embrace the whole of life, both good and bad, beauty and pain. "Acting isn't easy," she admits, "the rejection, the pressure. But it's my dream, so I take the challenges with the rewards. It sounds silly,"—she smiles—"but I prepare for luck."

"And luck found you." I smile. "Prepared."

"Yes!" She laughs.

It's funny, because it's true. Through perseverance, Lou reached this role and its sizeable payday.

"How do you feel?" I ask.

"It hasn't fully hit me," she says, "but I've relaxed. I'm letting go of perfectionism, people-pleasing."

"How freeing." My shoulders drop.

"Hopefully, it stays this way." She crosses her fingers.

"We need a standard," I relate. "To keep us on track."

"Agreed." She takes a sip of wine; she lights up. "Leonard Cohen dinner party."

"Go on . . ."

Lou continues, "We stay kind to all, but we check ourselves: *Does this feel like a dinner party hosted by Leonard Cohen? Am I being nourished? Am I nourishing others?* If yes, we invest time, energy. If no, we bless and move on."

"Yes." I'm at ease with her standard. "Hydra vision," I add.

"Hydra vision." She finishes her wine.

Dessert arrives. Banoffee pudding. We receive two shot glasses, each layered with toffee crunch, dulce de leche, banana, chocolate, cream.

Divine.

After dinner, Hollywood, where we meet Isla, Wallace at a Victorian house. The bouncer guides us inside, upstairs. We enter a bordello-style bedroom, and behind us, the door closes. In the corner, a woman reclines on the bed. And though we know what follows, we enjoy her show. It begins with a dimming of lights, then, jazz drum and striptease. At the height of her routine, she pulls a bedpost, her bed slides away, and she reveals a hidden staircase.

A speakeasy.

Once invited, we descend through the house into a courtyard. Lou recognizes friends. They have a table, so we join. Wallace knows one of them; they were together in Madrid. Isla knows another; JD shot him for a billboard. It's a small Hollywood world, and our groups merge. Pleased, I sit on a tufted leather sofa. Lou takes my side. On our left, two men engage us.

"Effortless," the first says.

"Pardon?" I ask.

"Your entrance," the second adds.

"Thank you," I say.

We continue talking. Lou excuses herself, for a call. One man leaves for the restroom. The other stays with me.

"What do you do?" he asks, his leg tapping.

"I'm a writer."

"TV? Movies?" He pours himself straight vodka; he starts vaping.

"Novels."

His interest wanes; I swivel the spotlight.

"And you?"

"I'm a director."

I think of Harry; I smile. "In my experience, directors are cool."

"I also study philosophy," he says.

Ding. Philosophy. I consider the merits of light mental sparring, when Lou returns.

"David Bowie!" she shouts to the music. And contacted by her high, I stand on the sofa, despite the Director's demand, "What are you doing?"

"My thing," I answer, reaching for Lou.

"Are we allowed?" she asks. Raised by rockers, her rebellion consists of immaculate etiquette.

"Go for it!" Wallace and Isla encourage.

"Alright . . ." Lou plants her red booties; she faces me, and we sing to Bowie.

"Let's Dance."

In front of the sofa, Wallace, Isla join our fun. And standing by the fireplace, a man observes. I whisper to Lou, "That's one of the owners."

"Are we in trouble?" she worries.

"No . . . I know him . . . I think."

"Think?"

"They're identical twins. I know one. . ." I say, when he waves, so I wave. "All good!" I hug Lou.

We sing; we dance through the song's end, when the Owner approaches. He's in black boots, black jeans, black hat, with a denim shirt, slightly unbuttoned. Without reproach, he extends a hand, helping us down.

"Hey!" I smile. We hug.

"How are you?" the Owner asks.

"Wonderful. You?"

"Can't complain. What are you drinking?"

"Whiskey."

"Your friends?"

"Same."

"Follow me." He leads us out of the courtyard, as I make introductions.

"What do you ladies do?" he asks.

"Actor," Lou.

"Agent," Isla.

"Producer," Wallace.

"Novelist." I savor the word.

"Whiskey bosses." He smiles.

"Exactly," Wallace says.

We climb stairs to a private bar. "I'm a collector," the Owner explains, browsing his bottles. "Since we have a writer in the house." He pulls something dated; he shows me the label.

"They trace this to Ernest Hemingway," he says.

"That's how we met!" I squeeze his arm. "Our love of Hemingway."

He starts laughing. "You think I'm my brother. That's his thing."

I blush.

"Fifty-fifty chance?" Isla defends me.

"But you hugged me!" I say. "The hug's how I tell. Why'd you hug me?"

"Your energy," he says.

I pull my hands to my heart. "Oh."

"Now, you know both brothers." Lou smiles.

"Exactly," the Owner says.

He pours five glasses.

"Kind calls to kind," he toasts. Then, we sample a pour from Papa Hemingway.

Neat.

Back on the sofa, the Director saved my seat.

"What's it about?" he asks.

"Pardon?"

"Your novel."

"Life."

"Ha," he huffs, still vaping, still tapping his leg. "Life is meaningless."

Quite broody, he dives into darkness, waxing woefully about the fall of man, God being dead. He's my polar opposite, which fascinates me, so I buckle in; I listen. Without being challenged, he slows his roll, so I chime in. "I hear you. We may never identify life's meaning. That's why I'm a happy existentialist."

"Sounds made up," he snarks.

"It is. That's the point. It's on us to give life meaning."

"Huh." He's intrigued. "What's yours?"

I cross my legs. "Beauty. Love. Art. Peace. *Enjoyment*. Personally, I'm banking on God, the essence. A higher consciousness, including you, me . . ." I open my arms to the night. "This." I shake my arms. "Why not embrace the mystery?"

He stops vaping. "How do you take yourself seriously?"

"I don't. I used to . . . but it was a fucking bummer. So, I changed my mind. As I did, I unlocked this high, like you wouldn't believe. I'm not always there, but I'm starting to stay . . . longer."

He cracks his knuckles; I think: *Leonard Cohen dinner party*. I'm about to leave, but before I go, I ask, "Do you consider yourself happy?"

"Not at all."

"Maybe," I dare, "it's time for a new philosophy?"

He's taken aback.

Lou checks in. "Everything OK?"

"Your friend's blowing my mind," the Director says.

"She does that." Lou laughs.

"Seems I've got a shit world view," he tells her. "Any suggestions?"

Lou reaches for her wallet. "Actually, yes."

Surprising him, surprising me, she unfolds a page, torn from a book. "*Dance Dance Dance*," she says, "Haruki Murakami." After smoothing the words, she clears her voice.

"*Dance,' said the Sheep Man.*

"*Yougottadance. Aslongasthemusicplays. Yougottadance. Don'teventhinkwhy. Starttothink, yourfeetstop. Yourfeetstop, wegetstuck. Wegetstuck, you'restuck. Sodon'tpayanymind, nomatterhowdumb. Yougottakeepthestep. Yougottalimberup. Yougottaloosenwhatyoubolteddown. Yougottauseallyougot.*

K. E. GREGG

Weknowyou'retired, tiredandscared. Happenstoeveryone, okay? Justdon'tletyourfeetstop.'"

Silence.

Lou and I look at the Director. Visibly, he spins his wheels. We wait. Patient. Hopeful. For . . . *epiphany.* Something clicks.

"Feed the cut," he says.

"Yes!" Lou agrees.

To my blank stare, he elaborates. When directing, he must focus the actors, the dialogue, the action in a way that feeds each frame to propel the desired plot. Good direction makes good movies. While talking, his epiphany enriches. "Fuck. I'm the director of my life. You're the author of yours."

"Wow, that's spot on," I connect.

His demeanor changes; he's open, smiling. I give him a hug, and I repeat his line.

"Feed the cut."

93

REVIEW.

Another birthday approaching, I peruse my journals. On one page, I marvel at something I noted.

Aldous Huxley: *"It's extraordinary the way the whole quality of our existence can be changed by altering the words in which we think and talk about it."*

Absolutely.

94

HEAVEN.

The Rolling Stones play from Lou's iPhone. Soft, sweet, psychedelic. "Heaven." An ethereal hype song.

As I dance toward her, she presents a confetti cake.

"Happy birthday!"

We grab coffee in Venice, then we walk along the beach to Santa Monica. Near the Casa del Mar Hotel, we stop at a bench. As we sit, I notice a plaque, "*Make the best of this life.*" I trace the plaque; Lou lights golden candles. When the cake's aglow, she holds it out, and in place of a wish, I choose appreciation.

Thank you.

Over cake, coffee, we watch the beach, the waves, and my mind takes on a rhythm. *Thank you. Thank you.*

Soon, the rhythm gives way to revelation.

We give. We receive. We give. We receive. If we remain open, it balances. We become nourished, while nourishing.

After breakfast, Lou has a photo shoot, so she walks me home. *Om mani padme hum.*

At my doorstep, we hug.

"Thirty-seven!" she cheers.

"Here we go . . ."

Hours later, a knock.

Golden heart balloons, from Isla. When the deliveryman hands them to me, I decide to take a walk with my gift. It's childlike, but I adore how balloons float and twist in the air. *Om mani padme hum*, I think, as I pass a nearby house. At the gate, I pause. I stare up at the tree. In a few weeks, it will turn purple. Jacaranda. For now, I inhale climbing garden roses.

"Peace," a man says.

"Peace," I answer, innately, as he approaches.

"That rose," he clarifies, "it's called Peace."

"Beautiful." I smile, and the man seems to recognize me.

"Wait. It's you! Please don't go anywhere; I'll be right back."

"OK." I smell the roses.

Minutes later, he returns with another man. "This is my husband," he explains.

"I've been wanting to thank you," the Husband says, moving slowly, yet brightly, with a cane.

"Me?"

"You."

The Husband taps his cane; he shares his story. For years, he had been wheelchair bound. Like that, he spent mornings, at his desk, facing the window. One day, he noticed me, walking. Few people distract him, but for some reason, he watched me, intently.

"You looked so happy," he says. "Simply, happy, walking."

Day after day, he awaited my arrival. "Like clockwork." And though he'd given up hope, one day, he decided, "I will walk again." On that phrase, the Husband raises his silver lion-topped cane. "Look at me now."

"What a story . . ." I sigh.

"Thank you," he says. "We are forever grateful. Is it your birthday?" He notes the balloons.

"It is."

"Hearts of gold, eh? Neil Young fan?"

"I am."

"Me too. Happy birthday, dear."

"Thank you, your story is the perfect present."

"I'm glad. See you tomorrow?"

"See you tomorrow."

I walk on.

Ripples. I'm casting ripples.

We give. We receive. We give. We receive.

Reciprocity.

Back home, I start a new journal.

Notes of the day's beauty.

As I write, a theory: *We're all angels.* Sometimes we lead. Sometimes we follow. At our best, we shine. When we do, we turn others on. Another thought flashes; I turn the page; I jot down a Japanese concept.

"From kensho *to* satori."

I close the journal.

By the balcony, my balloons catch sunlight. I reach for a book. A gift from Wallace, *Devotion* by Patti Smith. Once I start, I read it cover to cover. On page 93, I'm moved to tears.

"What is the dream? To write something fine, that would be better than I am, and that would justify my trials and indiscretions. To offer proof, through a scramble of words, that God exists."

I set the book down. *A shared dream.* Completely contented, I shuffle on music. It's Incubus. "Wish You Were Here." Brandon Boyd sings; I lay back.

Happy.

Here.

95

SWANS GLIDE THE LAKE.

It's April. After ballet, I visit an oasis, one that I discovered by way of Steve Jobs. Out of his biography, to Yogananda's *Autobiography of a Yogi*, to Lake Shrine. A sacred place, at the end of Sunset. Open to all.

Peaceful, I walk the lake. There's a mulch path, shaded by willowy flowering trees. Not a cloud in the sky. Only a few meditative passersby. At the waterfall, I read an engraved wooden sign. A passage from the Bhagavad Gita:

"He who perceives Me everywhere and beholds everything in Me never loses sight of Me, nor do I ever lose sight of him."

I hear Zion in my mind, *Everything*. I smile, aware that no religion, no label, nobody owns this force. This creative power. Flow. It resides within us. Around us. Everywhere.

Everything.

I continue. I enter an outdoor sanctuary for a date with Gandhi. Near the enshrined portion of his ashes, I sit. For a while, my eyes follow swans, gliding across the lake. Once composed, I speak.

"Gandhi," I say, as though he were present, "I did it. I finished my first manuscript. For peace." Then, I look to the sky. "We did it."

A few petals float from the trees onto my lap. I take them in my hands. No thoughts.

Only serenity.

96

"MAY I JOIN YOU?"

I'm pulled from my reading, *Windblown World,* a compilation of Jack Kerouac's journals.

"Zion!"

We hug; he takes a seat next to me at the bar. The bartender selects new vinyl for the turntable, and soon, Bob Marley & the Wailers.

"Three Little Birds."

To reggae, we receive hot towels, fragrant with frankincense, pine. On instinct, Zion and I inhale the scent; we close our eyes.

"How was D.C.?" he asks.

"Powerful," I say.

"The hero going home with the elixir." He grins.

"I don't think it's home anymore."

"I see," he says.

"Where do you consider home?" I ask.

He places a hand to his chest. "Here." Without thinking, I mirror him. "Welcome home," he says.

Reunited, we order lunch: pickles, sashimi, gyoza, hand rolls, a wagyu bowl. Then, *hōjicha*, a tea known for its fire-roasted leaves, a process born in Kyoto. Cradling a coarsely glazed mug, I tell Zion about the shadows I faced in D.C.

"You're human," he says. "We all experience pain. And sometimes, that pain gets re-triggered. When you stay present, when you face it, it dissolves. One day . . . you're no longer triggered."

"Here's to that." I sip my tea.

Conversation continues; we share blood orange sorbet. It's rich yet refreshing, and I'm cooled by each bite from a tiny wooden spoon.

Now, we're discussing detachment.

"Not only from pain." Zion spins his rings. "From joy."

"Detach from joy? What about your dream wave?"

"Especially my dream wave. I value it, so I surrender it. There's no way I can control when or how or if it will arrive, all I can do is prepare. Otherwise, I'd go mad."

"Great white whale," I say.

We laugh.

"Detach from my dreams," I repeat the wisdom.

"Or, hold your dreams gently. I've found that life declares itself, when you give it space."

I make a mental note. We finish with drinks, spiked kombucha. And when the bill arrives, Zion pays.

"Thank you," I say.

"Treat me to some of that book?" he asks, signing the check.

"Happily. Want to play my favorite game?"

"For sure."

"OK." I pass him the book. "Open it at random; see where your eyes land. Kerouac will tell us what we're meant to hear."

Zion follows the instruction. His tanned, freckled face smiles. Then, he reads aloud.

"APRIL 1949. ROAD-LOG. THURS. 28 . . . *It appears I must have been learning . . . my prose is different, richer in texture.*"

At this point, Zion strengthens his voice, *"What I've got to do is keep the flow, the old flow, nevertheless intact."*

"Of course." I beam. A win. For me. For Zion. For today, April 28, 2018.

Keeping the flow.

97

A CONCERT.

Many concerts. A two-day festival.

I open my eyes before my alarm. I relish sateen sheets, a hot shower, a Turkish towel. Simple pleasures. Gateways to goodness. I dress in cutoffs and a bodysuit. My iPhone chimes, "I'm here," so I drape a jacket around my shoulders. Day sequins. À la Salvador Dalí.

For the way they play with light.

Out front, a black Escalade.

I climb into the back seat, next to Lou.

"You did it!" She hugs me.

"I did."

Years of writing, complete. A final draft. A manuscript.

"Happy summer!" she says.

"What timing that you're on break from filming."

"Meant to be."

Catching up, we make our way to Arroyo Seco, a laid-back foodie music festival, on golf course greens. We arrive for Seu Jorge. With horns and drums, the Brazilian artist strums his guitar, massaging my spirit. In Portuguese. High on life, I shimmy, my sequins catching sunshine.

Later, Jack White, staged in royal blue. What he does with his guitars . . . his drums . . . it's gospel. Not church, but soul. More than music—a way of being. My mind flashes to wisdom from Jack White about the connection between rock star appeal and freedom. More specifically, the freedom to express one's full range of experience. Up. Down. Dark. Light. One big party. A rampant demonstration of life. As I marinate on these insights, his set builds to "Seven Nation Army." My high grows higher.

"We can have it all," I tell Lou.

"Hydra vision." She dances.

Before Neil Young, we head for beer. In line, my heart skips. It's a Duke guy. Friends with my ex-husband. Former friends with me. I'm triggered, which means opportunity. I breathe. I do nothing. I expect nothing. My heart settles. From that place, I invoke a positive memory.

"See that guy ordering?" I ask Lou.

"I do."

"Want to hear a story?"

"I do."

I describe a beach day, Red Hot Chili Peppers blasting, a heated game of beer pong, socks on cocks. Ridiculous. Carefree.

"Were you wearing your captain's hat?" Lou asks.

"Of course." I laugh.

"Even though you aren't her anymore," she says, "we can still love her."

"*Thank you*." I hug Lou; I make peace.

We reach the front. Lou orders Peronis. I take a sip, and I hear, "Gracie?"

It's Duke Guy, with a giant hug. "You look great."

"Thank you," I say. "This is Lou."

"What've you been up to?" he asks me.

"It's been years." I raise my beer, unsure how to answer, when Lou saves me. "She wrote a novel."

"Wow," Duke Guy says. "About what?"

"Life." I smile.

"Am I in it?" he asks.

"Not yet." I laugh. "But it's nice to see you."

"You too."

We hug good-bye; he walks away, then he turns back, "Gracie?"

"Yeah."

"If I were writing a novel . . . about your life . . . I would make sure it includes one phrase."

I'm surprised.

"Really?" I ask.

"Yes."

Then, I'm shocked. With all the sweetness in the world, he tells me, "*Buenas Ondas.*"

Good Vibrations.

98

MORE.

Still floating from last night, from Neil Young and Promise of the Real, we're back. Day two, Arroyo Seco. It's hot. Breezy and hot. I'm wearing a minidress that I bought in Mykonos. Life is good.

During golden hour, Gary Clark Jr. performs, and near the stage, I spot a mirage . . . no, it's him. *Tall dark rocker guy,* the Captain from the vines, Napa. Across the crowd, we make eye contact. I wave. He comes to me, and we hug.

"How do you know each other?" Lou asks.

"He serenaded me in Napa," I say.

"That seems right." Lou laughs.

"I'd love you to meet my band," the Captain tells me, so we combine forces.

Beers, laughter, and soon, we're hungry.

"Kogi?" I suggest.

"Their short-rib burrito makes me want to scream," Lou jokes.

"Done." The Captain leads the way.

Burritos in hand, we picnic in the grass, as skies turn pink over Pasadena. That's when it happens. A major life event. The act I'd been waiting for—Robert Plant. The man, the myth, the lead singer of Led Zeppelin. Though the band no longer performs, their front man could bring me close. Sensing my excitement, our rockers form a circle, holding space for me and Lou. What would transpire next? With Robert Plant in the flesh, who knew?

On my final bite of Kogi, it begins. A taste of Zeppelin, "The Lemon Song."

It's unreal. Robert Plant's as cool as you want him to be, and his voice casts a spell. Mesmerized, I unlace my espadrilles to dance barefoot in the grass. For me, it's transcendent. Six songs accompany the setting sun, into lucky number seven, "Going to California." Iconic Zeppelin. Ecstatic, Lou and I twirl.

"*Life!*" Lou cheers.

"Let's 'suck out all the marrow'," I quote Thoreau.

I clasp my hands to my chest, then I hug myself, *Here's to the mystery*. Never did I imagine this moment, and yet, here I am. Dancing. Five more songs, into the finale. A medley, with "Whole Lotta Love."

"Thank you!" I shout. To the heavens. The music ends; the festival bursts into applause; Robert Plant exits the stage. *What a high*, I inhale for posterity. As I do, my phone buzzes. It's Alexander. "Back in L.A."

"Where?"

"Pasadena."

"Me too!"

"I had a feeling. I'm playing a party. It's a gorgeous estate; bring friends."

"Now?"

"Now. The more, the merrier. Just send names for the list."

I confer with Lou, the Captain.

"Let's go!" Lou twists her hair into a bun. "My driver can take us."

"You in?" I ask the Captain, his band.

"Yes."

And so, we cross the golf course to the parking lot, where we pile into the Escalade. As we make our way to the party, I text friends, and with each reply, I notify Alexander, who confirms, "All set."

"We good?" Lou asks.

"Great." I smile.

On that, she rolls down the window. "Here we come."

GOLD.

Grateful, I smile at the color of Champagne in my coupe glass. *Gold.*

"Over here!" I shout to Isla.

"Hey babe!" She waves.

I'm standing by the pool, in the midst of idyllic grounds, surrounded by lush trees. The estate is more than gorgeous; it's a romantic Eden, complete with rose garden, waterfall, stream. When Isla reaches me, she's with Wallace, Hawk. Big hugs all around, and Isla says, "We walked in with Easton! He's in the house with your surfer friends."

Zion. Nate.

"I heard motorcycles," Hawk adds. "Is Moses coming?"

"He is!"

"It's going to be a night," Wallace says.

"It is!" Isla cheers.

"Come meet Alexander." I bring them to the DJ booth. Quickly, everyone connects.

"What an estate," Wallace says.

"Make sure to see the library." Alexander smiles.

"Nice." Hawk ties up his dreads.

"Thank you," Isla tells Alexander. Then, Wallace whispers something in his ear.

I'm about to ask, when Alexander gives me a hug. "Enjoy."

After visiting the library, I rally our group near Alexander.

It's Lou, the Captain, his band, Isla, Hawk, Wallace, Easton, Zion, Nate, Moses and crew. Soon, Jack arrives from Echo Park. He hugs me off my feet; I giggle. Overjoyed. On a whim, I'm celebrating with friends from prep school to present. We mix; we mingle. It's wild, yet meaningful. At one point, I introduce the Captain to Alexander. Together, we share stories. Then, Moses beckons, so I leave the music men alone; I rejoin the group. Next thing I know, Zion hands me a box of sparklers. "Take one, pass it on." Across the property, every guest receives a sparkler. As this happens, I notice Alexander give the Captain a mic; my heart races; Alexander spins the Captain's now-famous hit.

The Captain sings.

"Dream come true?" Jack places his arm around me, and we reminisce about my first time hearing this song. "Yes." I smile. We hug; we laugh; and everyone ignites sparklers. It's remarkable. Blazing, twinkling light.

Amazed, I go to Isla. "Wow." I sigh, admiring . . . *everything*. In response, she congratulates me. "See, babe? You created a new life for yourself. It's beautiful."

I pause. I nod.

We paint the night with our sparklers.

When the sparklers fade, the music changes. Immediately I laugh, and I look to Alexander, who places his hand to his heart. There's a tingling up my body. Wallace exclaims, "My song request! For Grace!" Teary-eyed, I dance with her. It starts with Slash's guitar. Steven Adler picks up on drums. Plus, Duff McKagan, Izzy Stradlin, Axl Rose—Guns N' Roses.

"Paradise City."

Elated, I think of my novel.

This novel.

"Grace Elizabeth." Jack smiles. "You're glowing."

"I made it." I raise my arms to the night.

Once upon a time, I felt a void, and it terrified me—but I faced it. Then, I filled it. According to my own design. Years later, surrounded by people who see me, the true me, I am brimming with awareness. On that vibe, Easton wraps me in his arms. Close to him, I divulge, "That morning, at *Declaration*, this is what I envisioned."

"It's lovely," he says.

I kiss his cheek; I dance away, to the edge of our group, on my own. Staring up at a giant moon, I understand what the Sage meant by living in the City of Peace and Happiness. It's a feeling, a comfort. Pure freedom.

It's my Paradise City.

Within me.

I made it.

Home.

Thank you.

Acknowledgments

Thank you to Dan Gerstein for welcoming me to the literary world. Thank you to Julie Blattberg for believing in me and guiding me through the publishing process. Thank you to Bryan Edwards and Megan Luke Edwards for years of friendship, including the creative collaboration that made this novel possible. Thank you to my editor, Emily Heckman, and my copyeditor, Marina Padakis Lowry. Thank you to my proofreader, Rebecca Maines; my text compositor, Clea Chmela; and my ebook producer, Kevin Callahan. Thank you to Erica D. Klein, M. K. Sadler, Martina Nilsson, Alison Christian, and Brian Doherty for supporting my vision with your talents.

Thank you to the artists, leaders, musicians, philosophers, and writers in *Paradise City*. I cherish your work, and I hope to point the way for others to cherish your work.

Thank you to my family, friends, and everyone who has enriched my life by loving me, inspiring me, teaching me, encouraging me, laughing with me, crying with me, celebrating with me—and now, reading my novel.

This book is a dream come true.

We did it.

a
AMANT
HOUSE

A place for beautiful books.

Amant House is an independent publishing house established in 2021 by K. E. Gregg, for the love of books.

In French, *amant* means lover.

When founding Amant House, Gregg collaborated with industry experts whose experience includes: Cambridge University Press, Grove Press, HarperCollins, Macmillan, Oxford University Press, Random House, and Simon & Schuster. Guided by their knowledge, she developed a bespoke, entrepreneurial process that values intention, innovation, creative freedom, and social impact. This process came to life thanks to the support of family, friends, and the tremendous talent of Gregg's advisors, editors, and designers.

Amant House's premier release is *Paradise City* by K. E. Gregg. From there, Amant House will release more books in support of its mission: to foster the art and culture of reading.

CPSIA information can be obtained
at www.ICGtesting.com
Printed in the USA
LVHW091533200921
698273LV00005B/263